The phantom figure
pursued her...

Trudy awoke with a start. It had only been a dream, but she was filled with a premonition of some terrifying thing. The bedroom was in darkness, and she strained to hear any sound that might have awakened her.

At first there was silence. Then, softly but clearly, she heard a low moaning. Perhaps it was just the wind. After all, the castle was perched atop a cliff. But she had the eerie sensation of another presence in the room, and she reached out frantically to turn on the bedside lamp.

On the pillow next to her, Trudy saw the white, tormented face of her dead aunt, staring up into the shadows....

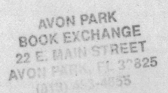

Books by Marilyn Ross

HARLEQUIN GOTHIC ROMANCE
11–SHADOWS OVER BRIARCLIFF

These books may be available at your local bookseller.

Don't miss any of our special offers. Write to us at the following address for information on our newest releases.

Harlequin Reader Service
901 Fuhrmann Blvd., P.O. Box 1397, Buffalo, NY 14240
Canadian address: P.O. Box 603,
Fort Erie, Ont. L2A 9Z9

CASTLE MALICE

MARILYN ROSS

Harlequin Books

TORONTO • NEW YORK • LONDON
AMSTERDAM • PARIS • SYDNEY • HAMBURG
STOCKHOLM • ATHENS • TOKYO • MILAN

To my good friends Dot and Bill Swangren

Published September 1986
ISBN 0-373-32012-4

Printed in Canada

CHAPTER ONE

SHE REALIZED SUDDENLY that she was alone on the railway platform. The few passengers of the high-speed express train who had joined her in getting off at the village of Palina had vanished. Even the uniformed railway attendant was nowhere in sight. Panic showed on her lovely round face, and her blue eyes were wide with apprehension as she gazed about her.

Moments earlier, she had been struck by the smallness of the station and the fine view it offered of the bay stretching out before it. All along the route the sleek steel train had kept close to the coast, and she'd had a wonderful panorama of the sea on one side and the distant mountain slopes on the other.

But now all Trudy Stone noticed was the eerie silence. Even the brilliant bougainvillea on the walls of the railroad station could not dispel her sense of gloom. There was simply no one in sight. She stood there forlornly with two pieces of luggage at her feet, her close-cropped blond hair and her slim, green-suited figure making her seem younger than her twenty-three years.

On a sudden decision, she went over to the station entrance—only to find it locked, with the padlock plainly in view. This had to mean the railway attendant had gone as well, leaving her with no access to a telephone or no one to consult. She searched the nearby grounds and saw a winding road. But if there were any houses on it, they were well out of sight.

Why had no one been there to greet her? She had been summoned to this village on the Italian Riviera by Giuseppe Pascal, who was her late aunt Julia's lawyer. He knew Trudy was arriving on this train, so surely some accident must have prevented him from coming. She was a stranger to Italy; actually, she had never left the United States until now. As she gazed at the lonely road, thick with trees on either side, she prayed that someone would come for her soon. She was terrified at being abandoned in this fashion.

In an attempt to keep her fear at bay, Trudy looked again at the distant sea. Its placid blue water was sprinkled with a myriad of pleasure craft. This different world had suddenly been opened up to her when she'd received a letter from Pascal, informing her that Julia LeBlanc, her mother's sister and her only aunt, had suffered a heart attack while swimming in her pool and had been found dead. As the nearest relative, Trudy had inherited Julia's entire fortune.

At first she had found it hard to believe. Her aunt had married and gone to Europe when she was a young woman. She had got divorced and then married a very wealthy French businessman. That was all Trudy knew about her. She had learned these sparse facts from her mother. After her mother died, she had received a brief note of sympathy from Julia, but her father had insisted that she not answer it. His position was that Julia had shown little interest in Trudy or his wife before, and he'd scorned her concern.

Trudy had not felt that way, but she'd obeyed her father's wishes. She was an only child, and at the time, they'd had a strong link between them. But that link had been broken when her father had met a woman of some means and gone off to California with her. Trudy had been heartbroken by her father's unexpected marriage and she had not liked her new stepmother. The dislike was evidently mutual, since she now heard from him only at rare intervals. There had been no invitations to visit.

Fortunately, she had a good job with a large New York insurance firm and shared a small apartment with another young woman from the office. Gloria Steel was Trudy's closest friend and confidante. It was to Gloria whom she'd first told the news of her legacy.

"What should I do?" she'd asked as she sat holding the letter in a trembling hand.

Gloria, dark-haired and intense, had replied, "You have no choice. You'll have to ask for a leave of absence and go to Italy!"

"But suppose it all collapses?"

Gloria smiled and patted her on the shoulder. "At least you will have had the trip. This lawyer is willing to send you expense money as soon as you let him know what you'll require."

"My dad will be furious if I go."

"Let him be. You hardly hear from him anymore."

"I *am* pretty much on my own," Trudy admitted.

"So make your own decisions," Gloria said. Then with a teasing smile, she added, "Unless you're afraid of losing Walter by going."

Trudy felt her cheeks burn. "That's silly," she protested. "I've only dated Walter a couple of times. We're the most casual of friends."

"Lucky for you, you're not engaged like me."

"It's different with you and you know it. You're in love with Ralph."

"Guilty," Gloria said. "I admit it. But you have no reason to miss this chance of a lifetime."

"I know so little about Aunt Julia. She married someone fabulously rich and had an active social life. He died a few years ago, and since then she'd been at their villa in Palina. She loved to swim—I do know that—so can you imagine her dying in the pool? It's awful!"

"The lawyer will answer all your questions," Gloria assured her. "He'll probably be handsome and wonderful and will ask you to marry him!"

Trudy laughed. "He's probably a fat family man of fifty with five children and an equally fat wife!"

Their conversation had taken place more than a month ago. It was now late August, Trudy had arrived to meet Giuseppe Pascal, and he had not shown up.

Her feelings of foreboding had been heightened in Genoa, where she'd stayed overnight before taking the train to Palina. After dinner she had gone for a walk, anxious to explore what she could of the port city. She was doing some window shopping at an exclusive dress shop when she felt a touch on her arm. Startled, she turned quickly to find herself staring into the face of an elderly, sad-looking woman with a dark kerchief on her head and wearing a shabby black dress.

"Please, signorina, let me tell your fortune," the woman pleaded in broken English.

Trudy felt sorry for her and, managing a smile, said, "I really don't believe in such things."

"Signorina, I read the palm. It is a gift of my people. I charge little."

Because Trudy realized that the woman was doing this as an alternative to outright begging, she felt she ought to go along with her request. "Very well," she said, extending her right hand.

The fortune-teller took Trudy's hand and studied it in the light from the display window. "You have traveled a great distance," she murmured.

"Yes, I have," Trudy agreed lightly, thinking that fact would be obvious from her looks and speech. But she was willing to continue with the charade.

"You have come here for a purpose," the woman intoned. "But it will not be as you expect."

Despite her conviction that this was all a sham, Trudy's attention was caught. "What do you mean?"

Then the gypsy looked up, and tears began to stream down her lined face. Shaking her head, she gasped, "No, signorina, no! It is all darkness! I cannot say more!" She turned and ran off down the street, soon to be lost amid the parade of people.

Trembling, Trudy stared after her. She couldn't believe what had happened. The woman's prime purpose had been to get some money from her, but instead, the gypsy had run off in a seeming state of terror.

Trudy tried to dispel the fear that the incident had created. She told herself it was all nonsense, but a nagging voice at the back of her mind kept arguing that there must have been something in her palm to send the woman off like that. Had she seen Trudy's imminent death in the lines of her hand?

Not able to shake off her troubled mood, Trudy hurried back to the hotel. In the lobby she sought out the polite night manager, who she knew spoke excellent English, and told him her story.

"Most unusual," was his comment. "She was undoubtedly a gypsy. There are many around here. You were lucky she didn't try to snatch your purse and run off with it."

"I think she was honest. That's what bothers me. Do you believe there are people who can read palms?"

He shrugged. "It is an ancient art. I have known several intelligent persons to rely on it."

"Whatever she saw scared her and made her run away."

"Perhaps she saw a policeman nearby. The authorities don't encourage these gypsies. Or it could be she's merely a trifle deranged."

"You think that's possible?" Trudy grabbed at this straw as an explanation to ease her fears.

"Very likely some poor soul suffering a mental illness," the man said, obviously noting that this was what Trudy wanted to hear. "I would not let it worry me."

"Thank you very much," she said, relieved.

But the feeling of relief had not lasted for long. By the time she had reached her room, she was again wondering what grim danger might be awaiting her.

From then on, her peace of mind had vanished. She had made the train journey to Palina filled with fear, in spite of the fact that she was on her way to claim the fortune her aunt had left her. It should have been one of the happiest moments of her life....

She stood on the deserted railway platform, tensely wondering what might happen next and worrying why the lawyer had not yet arrived to meet her. Surely this was not a good omen.

Then she heard the sound of a car approaching. She immediately felt better and watched the road expectantly. A sleek white convertible appeared around the bend. The driver, wearing dark glasses, brought the big sports car to a tire-squealing halt in front of the station and jumped out. He removed his glasses and came toward her.

He was a tall man, dark-haired, very tan and with strong features. A brown paisley ascot set off his expensive-looking beige silk jacket and brown slacks. He extended his hand to Trudy and smiled pleasantly. "So sorry to keep you waiting," he said. "There was an accident along the way, and I was held up."

Trudy was fascinated by his attractive appearance and his ability to speak English so well. "I was getting worried. You must be Signor Pascal."

The man's gray eyes twinkled. "I'm afraid not. I'm not even Italian. But I do happen to be a friend of Giuseppe Pascal's, and he asked me to meet you. I'm American, and my name is Dr. Carl Redman."

She shook her head. "I'm not sure I understand."

He laughed. "It isn't all that complicated. When Giuseppe arranged for you to arrive on this train, he didn't know he was going to be invited to an important house party in Lerici. Since he'll be there for several days, he asked me to meet you instead."

"I see," she said, not quite sure that she did. "I only know him from his legal letterhead."

"You will find him most amiable," Dr. Redman promised her. "He recently took over his father's law practice, but he'd been a playboy for so long, he's finding it hard to change his ways."

"Is he a young man?"

"Young and charming. And I feel sure that one day he'll be the equal of his late father as a legal expert."

"My aunt Julia must have had great faith in him."

"She did." He studied her for a moment. "So you are Trudy Stone. It's good to meet an American girl fresh from the States."

"You must meet many Americans here."

"Not all that many. We live fairly quietly. I'm employed as medical doctor and companion to the millionaire art collector Benson Steiburn. He has a castle practically next door to your aunt's villa."

"Interesting," she said. She was beginning to think that this tall American was much more complex than he appeared to be. "Are my aunt's servants still at the villa?"

"No," the young doctor said. "Giuseppe closed the place a month ago because there was a robbery. He felt some of the servants might have been mixed up in the theft, so he dismissed them."

This news, so casually offered, along with the fact that the lawyer had not thought it important enough to be there to greet her, sent Trudy into a distressed state of mind once again.

"What am I to do?" she asked. "Where am I to stay? Is there an inn?"

"None suitable," he said. "But have no fear. You are to be the guest of my employer. Mr. Steiburn will not hear of your staying anywhere else. His castle, as I have told you, is only a short way from the villa."

"It wouldn't be fair of me to impose on him," she protested. "I'm a complete stranger to him."

Carl Redman laughed easily. "But your aunt was one of his best friends. She was also a dear friend of mine. We often went swimming together. It was her favorite sport."

"You both knew her well?"

"She was at the castle much of the time. Her only other close friend was Lena Morel, an actress who lives in a cottage on the other side of the villa. The three places are rather isolated from the rest of the community."

Trudy was embarrassed. "I don't know what to say."

"Say nothing," was his advice. "Just come along with me. Is this all of your luggage?" He indicated the two suitcases.

"Yes."

He picked up the luggage and went to the car. Trudy followed him. After he had put the bags in the trunk, he opened the passenger door for her. "Now we'll be on our way."

The warmth of Carl Redman's personality made Trudy forget her fears. She was also entranced by the beauty of the Italian countryside. Between the distant blue mountains and the sea was an area of scenic delight. She marveled as Carl pointed out lemon and orange trees, banana plants, rose gardens, grape vines and the colorful bougainvillea that carpeted almost every stone wall.

"They call this the Riviera of Roses," he told her.

"It deserves the name," she agreed.

They drove through a tiny old town with several narrow streets, a few shops and a palm-tree-covered promenade.

"We are near both Portofino and Lerici," Carl said.

Trudy frowned slightly. "Those names sound familiar."

"You attended your English classes, that's why." He smiled. "The poet Shelley was drowned in the waters close by here. His body was washed ashore and then burned in a funeral pyre by his wife and companions. Both historians and romantics come here to spend a little time."

"So that's why I remembered the names," she said, enjoying his comments.

"In a few minutes we'll be reaching the cliffs on which the castle, Julia's villa and Lena's cottage are situated. By the way, our castle is called Castle Malice. Don't let that bother you—it's actually a most pleasant place."

"Then why the name?" she wanted to know.

"Goes back to the old days," he told her. "I'll explain later."

As they drove on, Trudy was amazed at and pleased by the relaxing influence that this charming stranger had on her. Studying his attractive profile, she decided he was probably in his early thirties. Her curiosity about him deepened.

"You say you are a medical doctor. Why on earth did you leave your practice to become a companion and physician to Benson Steiburn?"

Carl smiled. "Everyone asks me that. Steiburn was a patient at the American Hospital in Paris. I was doing a year there as an intern. He asked me to join him when I finished. I liked him and I shared his interest in art, so I decided it might be a rewarding job. And it has been."

"Is he a partial invalid?"

"No. Aside from having a slight heart condition, he's a very healthy man. My chief duty is to work with him on the purchase of paintings. He relies on me a lot."

"But you were trained to be a doctor!" Trudy could not restrain her outburst.

Carl nodded good-naturedly. "And I shall return to medicine. Just now I'm getting a life experience I couldn't find anywhere else."

"Does this millionaire have a family?"

"Only one daughter. Sylvia is married to a man who looks after Steiburn's business interests in New York. She's at Castle Malice now for a few week's holiday."

Trudy laughed. "Castle Malice! I'm dying to find out what's behind that somber name."

They rounded a corner and went up a small grade, and all at once she saw the castle. It was huge and of gray stone, covered with vines and topped by four round turrets. Nearby was a smaller stone building, still ample in size, with balconies and an imposing wide entrance. Just beyond it was a well-tended stone cottage with a thatched roof. All three structures looked out onto the sea from their high vantage on the cliff.

"They are just as you described them," Trudy said, studying the buildings with excitement.

"Mr. Steiburn and his daughter are waiting to greet you. I'm sure you'll be happy with us until Pascal can arrange for the villa to be opened."

"It's very good of them to have me."

As they drove up to the main entrance of the castle, she was struck by the magnificent rose gardens on either side of the broad steps. Their heady fragrance filled the air, and their colorful blooms added to the beauty of the surroundings.

Carl saw her up the front steps and into the dark, high-ceilinged hallway. Then he led her into an enormous living room that was decorated with fine antique furniture and whose walls were lined with paintings by the masters.

A thickset man with thinning white hair brushed straight back and a beard that jutted out aggressively came toward them, a pretty, dark woman trailing behind him. The man's gold-rimmed glasses gave his pale blue eyes a shrewd look. He wore an expensive white suit and, for Trudy's benefit, an expansive smile.

Offering her his hand, he said, "My dear Miss Stone, so you have arrived at last. I was one of your aunt Julia's dearest friends."

"It's so kind of you to invite me to stay here, Mr. Steiburn," Trudy said shaking hands with him.

"Under the circumstances, I can do no less." Then he turned to the young woman behind him and introduced her. "This is my daughter, Sylvia."

Sylvia smiled at Trudy and told her, "You know, you look a little like your late aunt. But, of course, she had reddish hair."

"You are a gorgeous blonde," Benson Steiburn chuckled. "You will get plenty of attention here in Italy, Miss Stone. There is a shortage of beautiful blondes."

Trudy smiled. "I never really expected to see Italy."

"Then your aunt's tragic death has done some small good. We all miss Julia. It was a bad business."

"I know little of what happened," Trudy admitted.

"No one else seems to know very much, either," Sylvia said. "She was found dead in the pool."

"The local doctor is old and has a language problem," Steiburn explained, "but we gathered from his report that she had a heart attack and drowned before help could come."

"Lena Morel was staying with her for a few days," Sylvia said. "She went out and found her in the pool. Then she came running over to us in a state of hysteria."

Carl Redman cleared his throat. "I've had Miss Stone's things sent upstairs."

"Fine." The millionaire turned to his daughter. "Sylvia, show Miss Stone her room."

"I'll be glad to," she said with a smile. "Come with me, Trudy."

"Thank you both for your help," Trudy told Carl and her host as she left them standing side by side in the living room.

She followed Sylvia up a winding, lushly carpeted stairway. Everything about the stone castle reflected good taste, yet in a lavish fashion.

"How is it in New York?" Sylvia asked over her shoulder.

"Still quite warm."

"I'm anxious to get back." The young woman sighed. "My husband is there. We have a place on Park Avenue."

Trudy was impressed. "That's a wonderful place to live."

"You'll like the villa when it's opened," Sylvia promised. "It's not as large as the castle, but it's beautifully furnished and twice the size of most villas here."

They reached the second landing, and Trudy was at once struck by a painting that dominated the wall there. It was a portrait of a masked swordsman in a black, flowing cape. She stood before it and exclaimed, "What a striking study!"

Sylvia smiled. "I'm not surprised you noticed it. It *is* different. The man in that painting lived here a hundred and fifty years ago and was responsible for the castle's being called Castle Malice."

Trudy's eyes widened, and she studied the painting more closely. The mask on the man's face did not conceal the fact that he had cruel features. "What did he do?"

"He was a half-mad aristocrat who deliberately caused arguments so he could challenge his opponents to a duel. Since he was an expert swordsman, the outcome of the matches was never in doubt. He killed one man after another and was rumored to have poisoned the widow of one of his victims because she repulsed his efforts to make her his mistress. He became known as the Count of Malice."

Trudy was thrilled by the story. "What happened to him?"

Sylvia smiled and shrugged. "He grew older, as everyone does. And lost much of his skill, as many people do. He challenged one adversary too many and was so seriously wounded he died a few hours later. His ghost is supposed to haunt this castle and the whole countryside."

"Carl Redman told me there was a story connected with the place. Now I know what it is."

Sylvia led the way down a hall to a heavy oak door, which she opened. Trudy followed her inside to find herself installed in a large suite with a dressing room and a private bath. A balcony off a French window faced the sea.

"I hope you'll be comfortable here," Sylvia said.

"I'm at a loss for words," Trudy told her. "I'm used to a rather simple life-style. This is almost too much."

Sylvia showed quiet amusement. "My father hardly thinks it's adequate. But then his standards are different from those of most people."

Trudy stepped out onto the balcony and saw that she also had a good view of the villa and the swimming pool, which lay between the two buildings. Gazing down at the calm blue surface of the oblong pool, she felt a tiny shudder go through her. It seemed to have an air of evil about it. She was sure her reaction was silly, but that was what she felt.

Sylvia came out on the balcony to stand beside her. Quietly, she said, "You're thinking about the manner in which your aunt died."

Trudy knew there was no use in denying this. "Yes. The pool leaves me with a sinister impression."

"I understand. Neither Father nor I am completely satisfied that Julia's death was a natural one."

Trudy turned to Sylvia with a small gasp. "Are you saying she might have been murdered?"

Sylvia shook her head. "No. I'm merely saying we weren't satisfied."

"Was Dr. Redman here?" Trudy asked. "Surely he would be aware if there had been foul play."

"He was in Genoa overnight on an art mission for my father."

"But who—why?" Trudy asked in bewilderment.

"Please don't upset yourself needlessly," Sylvia said, touching her gently on the arm. "Give yourself a chance to decide after you know this place and its people better." She paused. "It is a strange place, and there are some strange people here."

CHAPTER TWO

TRUDY BUSIED HERSELF with the unpacking of her
bags. Sylvia had told her to come downstairs when she
was dressed for dinner. As it was close to dinnertime,
she worked rapidly to hang some things in the closet
and place the rest carefully in the ample dresser. The
activity gave her little chance to dwell on the somewhat alarming words that Sylvia had left with her.

The fact that her aunt's death was something of a
mystery put a different light on everything. She had
been told by Pascal that her aunt had died as a result
of a heart attack while swimming in the pool. It now
seemed that others were not as willing to accept this
explanation as he had been.

Trudy showered, donned fresh underwear, then
chose a simple white dress with string straps. Carefully checking her makeup, she touched it up a little
and gave her hair a final brushing.

As she descended the winding stairway, she heard
voices coming from the living room, so she went
straight in there. Steiburn, his daughter and Carl
Redman were standing with wineglasses in their hands,
talking to a slender blond man who looked rather
weary.

Benson came over to her with a warm smile. "You
look fabulous, my dear. I would like to introduce you

to Adrian Romitelli, who was a friend of Julia's and whom we all see a great deal of, since he rents a cottage near here.''

Adrian offered Trudy a thin smile as he took her hand. "A pleasure to meet you, Trudy. Your aunt and I played tennis often. Do you play?''

"I used to, a little," she said pleasantly. "I haven't for a while.''

"We must correct that soon," he said, showing just a trace of an accent in his suave voice.

"Don't allow him to bully you. He's tennis-mad," Carl put in.

Steiburn eyed the blond man and said, "You might say he does little else. He used to be an excellent concert pianist. Now he spends all his time here.''

Adrian's cheeks showed crimson. "I gave up my concert work because of an injured hand.''

"If you want to play tennis, Trudy," Sylvia said, "I'll let you have an outfit of mine. I'm sure everything will fit—we're almost the same size and weight.''

Adrian turned to Trudy. "So you will have no excuse not to play.''

"Perhaps after I get more adjusted to things here," she said.

Benson Steiburn brought her a glass of wine and told her, "Before we go in to dinner, I'd like to show you something in the library.''

He led her to another large room, located behind the living room. It was lined with bookshelves on two of its walls, and paintings hung on the paneled surfaces of the other two. He halted before a large portrait of a distinctive-looking woman whose red hair was pulled back from her oval face and tucked in a coil at the nape of her neck. She wore a magnificent string of pearls and a pale green dress.

"Your aunt Julia," the art collector said, sipping his wine. "I had it done two years ago. I wanted her to take it, but she insisted I keep it here."

"She was quite attractive," Trudy murmured.

"She was also very intelligent," the white-haired man said with a hint of sadness.

"Your daughter suggested that there were some unexplained things about her death."

The pale eyes behind the glasses blinked. "Sylvia is given to dramatic interpretations of events. She often makes too much of ordinary happenings. That's a flaw she inherited from her mother."

Trudy stared at him. "You're telling me there was no mystery about the way Aunt Julia died?"

He replied carefully. "Any death under such circumstances gives rise to speculation and gossip. I can only say the doctor who examined her seemed to be certain she had died from a heart seizure and subsequent drowning in the pool."

"She drowned, then?"

"Yes—after the seizure. It couldn't have happened otherwise. She was an excellent swimmer."

"I'm surprised there was no one there with her."

"There was. Sylvia told you earlier about Lena Morel. You'll be meeting her. She was with Julia that night and had been swimming, too, but had gone inside for a drink. She's inclined to drink too much these days. By the time she came out, she wasn't quite sober, and discovering your aunt lifeless in the pool gave her a nasty shock. She ran straight over here."

"Mightn't she have been able to save my aunt if she'd been with her at the time of her seizure?"

He nodded soberly. "Obviously one of the many speculations."

Trudy gazed up at the painting again. "Her lawyer gave me no hint of this," she said bitterly.

"Giuseppe Pascal is a strange fellow," Steiburn told her. "He is shrewd but at the same time a playboy. So he is often careless about his responsibilities."

"I found that out today," she said, thinking about being alone at the station.

"You will discover it's a habit with him." Steiburn tugged at his whiskers. "I dislike saying this, but he didn't close the villa soon enough, and as a result, four or five valuable works of art were stolen."

"Carl Redman told me that."

"What are your plans for the villa?"

"I haven't even thought about it."

"Your aunt was worried about its condition," he said. "Shortly before her death, she discussed the repairs it would need, and we both came to the same conclusion—that she should sell it and move to another, more modern home. There are some available nearer the beach."

"I certainly haven't had any experience with a house full of servants. And what would I do with all that space?"

"Exactly," Steiburn agreed. "I'd have Pascal give you a tour of it, then strip it of its furnishings and art and place them in storage until you find another place to live. You can put the villa up for sale."

"But I can't stay here," she protested. "I can't impose on you that way."

He laughed. "We have room for fifty like you. Sylvia and I are delighted to have company from home. Inspect the villa, but don't try to reopen it and live there. It might be dangerous for you to live there alone."

"Dangerous?" she echoed.

"'Unwise' is a better word," he amended hastily. "And now let's join the others and proceed to the dining room."

The dining room was as high-ceilinged as the other rooms she'd seen and had sparkling crystal chandeliers and rich wood paneling. They sat at a long table, all of them gathered at one end of it. The millionaire art collector sat at the head of the table, and Trudy and his daughter sat on either side of him. Next to Trudy was Adrian Romitelli; Carl was seated next to Sylvia.

The dinner proved to be as elaborate as the room. The service was discreet and prompt; entrée, a delicious fresh fish. Conversation touched on many things, especially art.

"Are you also interested in art, Trudy?" Adrian asked.

"I have only a casual knowledge of painting and painters," she admitted.

He said with an air of cynicism, "It would seem that you will automatically become the owner of a fairly important collection, whether you appreciate it or not. You won't be alone. Many collectors have a greed to possess and care nothing for what they have acquired."

Benson Steiburn gave the thin-faced young man a sharp glance. "I hope you don't include me in that group."

Romitelli's smile was cold. "Would you expect me to?"

"Father cares too much for his paintings, if anything." Sylvia spoke up like the dutiful daughter she was.

"I agree," Carl said. "Few people have a genuine love of art as Mr. Steiburn does."

"Thank you," Carl's employer replied flatly. With his eyes still on Romitelli, he continued. "I'd very much like to know who was responsible for taking those paintings from the villa. I don't think the servants were to blame, but I believe someone who knew the house engineered the theft."

There was a long moment of silence. Then Adrian smiled weakly and said, "So all of us, with the exception of Trudy, could be considered suspects. We all had access to the villa."

"So did other people, like Lena Morel," Sylvia put in hastily, clearly trying to avoid any embarrassing finger-pointing.

"It will come out in time," her father said, touching his napkin to his lips. That was the signal for them to leave the table. They rose, and Benson, Sylvia and Adrian headed for the living room. Trudy and Carl strolled along the hallway behind them.

"I'll show you some of the paintings," he said, "unless you want to join the others."

"I'd like a short tour," she told him with a smile. "I found the atmosphere at the table a trifle tense."

"My boss and Romitelli?" he said, amusement on his handsome face. "Mr. Steiburn has a rather poor opinion of that young man and doesn't worry about expressing it."

She looked up at him. "Is his prejudice warranted?"

"Romitelli has become a hanger-on. He lives by borrowing from friends. He owed your aunt a large sum of money, and when she asked him to pay some of it back, he laughed at her. She told me that herself."

"That shocks me."

"Prepare to be shocked further. This beauty spot along the Mediterranean is just a little short of being paradise."

"I'm starting to realize that."

His eyes twinkled. "Don't despair. There are some very nice people here. Now I'll show you a valuable Rousseau."

The painting was in a side room that Trudy thought might serve Benson Steiburn as a kind of office. The Rousseau was an excellent one, even to her untutored eye. She and Carl moved about the room as he showed her works by Chagall and Manet, and a very different and eye-catching modern painting by Dali.

Once again she lost her feeling of fear and unease in the company of the pleasant young doctor. They went into another room, and he pointed out and explained still more paintings. She found it hard to believe that he could be anything but her friend.

"Do you think it will be cold out?" she asked. "I'd like to stroll through the grounds in the moonlight."

"I'll find you a cloak," he said. A moment later he'd fetched one, probably from a nearby closet. She guessed it might belong to one of the maids, but it would do for a temporary protection.

They left the castle by a side door that faced the villa. A full moon had risen to brightly illuminate the immediate area, but the villa lay in darkness.

Involuntarily, Trudy grasped Carl's arm. "I have a strange feeling about that place. It looks so sinister. I think your employer is right—I should sell it."

"Did he tell you that?"

"Yes."

The doctor looked interested. "Perhaps he may want to buy it."

She gazed at him in surprise. "But he claims the place is in bad shape."

"I know, but he'd want to tear it down and build something practical. He'd like the location for a modern art museum for his collection."

"It's hard to imagine anyone having so much money!"

"Believe me, he manages it very well," Carl said wryly.

"I'm sure he does." She paused and realized they were strolling by the rose gardens, whose fragrance filled the night air. "Do you think Adrian Romitelli could have taken those paintings from the villa?"

Carl hesitated, then said, "I'd rather not give you a direct answer. But let me say he could be capable of it, should his position be desperate enough."

"And is it?"

"No one really knows. Still, we do know about his borrowing money."

"I guess Castle Malice is aptly named. So many dark things appear to be going on here."

Carl smiled. "It received its name long ago."

"I know all about it. Sylvia told the whole story."

They had reached the pool belonging to the villa. He halted and asked her, "Did she also warn you that the swordsman's uneasy spirit still haunts the castle and even as far as the village?"

"Yes."

"Many claim to have seen the ghost, and it's been blamed for all kinds of bizarre things."

"Have you seen it?"

"I think I may have. But perhaps it was only a shadow."

She looked down at the reflections of moonlight in the pool. "Do you think the swordsman's ghost might have caused my aunt's death?"

"It's strange you should ask that," he said.

"Why?"

"After Julia was found drowned, many people in the village blamed it on the curse of the masked swordsman. Of course, they're just ignorant, superstitious local folk."

"They might not be all that wrong," she said, her eyes still fixed on the pool. "Perhaps the ghost's wicked influence caused someone else to bring about her death."

He shrugged. "If we follow that line of thinking, maybe Julia saw the ghost and was frightened into a seizure."

"Speculation and gossip." She sighed. "I didn't come here expecting those things."

"You have my sympathy, believe me. Money isn't everything, as you are finding out. It's possible you were better off with your way of life back in New York."

"Perhaps I was."

"What about your personal life?" he asked. "Are you engaged, committed to anyone?"

She smiled and shook her head. "I have a few nice male friends. But no one special. I haven't been that lucky."

"I guess the right man hasn't come along yet."

"What about you?" she asked, gazing up into his face, which looked even more attractive in the flattering moonlight.

"I thought I was in love once," he replied quietly. "The girl married someone else, someone with power and more money."

A thought came to her, and she couldn't resist asking, "Was it Sylvia you were ready to marry?"

He nodded. "Yes. It seems ridiculous now. We're the best of friends, but we'd never have made it as husband and wife."

"So it turned out for the best."

"For both of us. The only one who was disappointed was her father, since he'd encouraged the match." Carl smiled bleakly.

"Is he a widower?"

"Yes. But he and his wife were separated for years before she died about five years ago. After that, he had the portrait of Julia painted. I thought he might actually ask her to marry him. Maybe he did. But nothing came of it."

"Perhaps she preferred her independence."

"She was a strong woman," he agreed. "And youthful for her age."

"I hope I'll soon see the lawyer and find out where I stand."

"I don't think he'll show up before the first of the week," Carl warned her. "In the meantime, I hope you'll allow me to help you in any way I can."

"Thanks," she said gratefully. "You have no idea how much I appreciate that. If it weren't for you, I'd be terrified by all this."

"Don't be afraid," he said gently and, without warning, took her in his arms and bestowed a light kiss on her lips.

Being in his arms seemed so right, the soft touch of his lips so satisfying, that Trudy offered no resistance. After a moment he released her.

"Forgive me," he apologized. "I didn't intend to do that. An impulse caught me off guard."

She smiled up at him and touched his arm. "It wasn't all that wrong an impulse."

His eyes widened. "Do you feel the same way I do? Is it possible we've both found something in each other?"

"It could be," she said softly. "Just as long as we don't try to rush things."

"I won't be guilty of that," he promised. "But I do want you to remember how I feel about you."

She laughed. "I'm not liable to forget. Now it's time to go back inside. They'll be wondering about us."

Once they'd returned to the castle, they joined the others in the living room. Adrian Romitelli came over to Trudy immediately and sat by her. "I want you to play tennis with me in the morning," he said.

"I haven't played in ages," she protested.

"Sylvia is going to supply you with everything. It will do you good."

"Perhaps," she hedged, hoping to get rid of him.

"I'll call for you at ten, then," he said quickly. "I'm leaving now. I really do want to see you tomorrow." The way he said this struck Trudy, as if he had something urgent to tell her.

Sylvia rose to see him on his way. "No need to worry, Adrian. I'll see she's outfitted and ready by ten." Then she left the room with him.

Benson Steiburn stood up with a smile and said, "Sylvia enjoys taunting that young scoundrel and invites him here more often than I like."

"It looks as if Trudy will have no choice but to play tennis with him," Carl remarked.

Steiburn chuckled. "Do me a favor, my dear. Beat him every set." He said good-night and strode off.

Carl sat down on the arm of Trudy's chair and took her hand in his. "Well, it's been quite a night for us, hasn't it?"

"It has," she agreed.

He grinned. "From the moment I saw you on the railway platform, I had a special feeling about you."

"I was more than glad to have *you* come along."

"I have to drive to Lerici on estate business tomorrow, or I'd play tennis with you myself, just to cut out Romitelli."

"He's harmless."

"Don't be too sure," he cautioned. "But better to play with him once, anyway. Then perhaps he'll get over his obsession and give you some peace."

"I'll play so badly he'll never want to have a game with me again!"

"Do that," Carl said. "And now I'll see you safely upstairs."

EXCEPT FOR A NIGHT LIGHT on the stand beside her bed, the big room was in shadows. A maid had turned down the bed and put out her nightgown. Trudy leaned against the door after she'd said good-night to Carl and found her mind in a whirl. So much had happened so quickly.

She was still apprehensive about the situation she found herself in because of her aunt Julia's legacy. From what she'd heard thus far, her fears were well taken. The questions about Julia's death, together with the bleak atmosphere of the villa, made her worry that worse revelations might await her.

On the credit side, there was the kindness of Benson Steiburn and his daughter, not to mention the warm friendship offered her by Carl Redman. She wondered if he had fallen in love with her just a little. It was such a delightful possibility she couldn't help but linger on it for a few moments.

She'd prepared for bed and was in her nightgown when she heard someone knock softly on the door. She glanced around, startled, then went over and asked, "Who is it?"

"Sylvia," came the woman's muffled voice from the other side of the heavy door.

"One moment," Trudy said. She unlocked and opened the door, and Sylvia entered, wearing a blue dressing gown and carrying tennis clothes, socks and sneakers in her hands.

She smiled. "I thought you'd want these for the morning."

"You shouldn't have bothered," Trudy protested.

"I'm only worried about the shoes," Sylvia said. "Try them on."

Trudy sat in an easy chair and put them on. Then she stood up and announced, "They fit fine!"

"Good! Now you really will have to play tennis with Adrian in the morning."

"I can't imagine why he's so anxious to play tennis with me."

"I can," Sylvia said with a knowing smile. "You're a pretty American girl about to inherit a lot of money—the kind of girl every Italian man dreams about for a wife."

"You're joking!"

"Not in poor Adrian's case." Sylvia shook her head. "His musical career got nowhere, and he isn't good enough at tennis to be a pro. So he's had to earn a living as a kind of gigolo. He borrowed money from Julia and thought it was a fair return for giving her his attention."

"Well, he mustn't get any ideas about me," Trudy said.

"If I were in your place, I'd be a lot more interested in Carl."

"He *is* very nice," Trudy agreed.

"I think so, too. My problem was that I was already engaged when I met him. It was too late for us."

Sylvia's words stunned Trudy. What she was saying was the opposite of what Carl had told her. According to his version, Sylvia had been engaged to him and left him for the man who was now her husband. But why would he have lied to Trudy about this?

"And you and Carl never were engaged?" she asked.

Sylvia laughed. "Never. So I offer him to you. It's easy to be generous when one has a happy marriage." She kissed Trudy on the cheek and said, "Have a good night's rest, and please my father by beating Adrian at tennis tomorrow."

Trudy summoned a faint smile in reply.

They said good-night, and she closed the door again. This time she found herself more confused than ever. Why had Carl tried to make her think that he and Sylvia had once been engaged? It really didn't concern her one way or the other. She'd never have thought anything about it.

But what really bothered her was the fact that he had lied to her. That the lie itself was not of importance didn't matter! It was the principle involved. Since he had lied to her about this, he could lie to her about other things—such as how he felt about her.

The darkness was closing in once again. Her fears began to return. She was in a foreign land, among strangers, with only their word to depend on. She had been deserted by the lawyer who was representing her and locked out of the villa that had been left to her. Now she found that her trust in the one person who had assumed importance to her had been misplaced.

Her eyes were filled with tears as she turned off the light and lay back on the pillows. It was a long while before her troubled thoughts allowed her to sleep. But her sleep was fitful, interspersed with dreams in which the phantom figure of the gypsy woman pursued her through dark underground rooms.

Trudy awoke with a start, her heart pounding, her breathing difficult. It was as if a cold chill had coursed through her. She was filled with a premonition of some terrifying thing. The room was in darkness, and she strained to hear any sound that might have awakened her.

At first there was only silence. Then softly but clearly, she heard a low moaning. Perhaps it was just the wind, she thought, which would surely play about this castle perched atop a cliff. She had the eerie sensation of another presence in the room, and she reached out frantically to turn on the bedside lamp.

On the pillow next to her, she saw the white, tormented face of her drowned aunt Julia staring up into the shadows.

CHAPTER THREE

WITHOUT GLANCING AT that white, haunting face again, Trudy let out a piercing scream. She sprang from the bed and ran to the door, jerked it open and then rushed out into the hallway, screaming again and again. Her cries for help were an almost automatic response to her shocking discovery.

The first person to appear was Benson Steiburn, wearing a dark dressing gown. He looked perturbed as he placed a reassuring arm around her. "What on earth is wrong, my dear?" he asked solicitously.

She closed her eyes and moaned. "I saw her! I saw her!"

"Saw who?" he asked more sharply.

"Aunt Julia," she replied. "In my bed!"

"You must have had a nasty nightmare," he said. When Sylvia came to join them a moment later, he told his daughter, "You stay here with Trudy while I look inside." And he left them.

Sylvia was clearly worried. "Whatever happened?"

"I think I saw a ghost," Trudy whimpered.

"What is this about ghosts?" Carl Redman stood there in pajamas and a robe.

Trudy stared at him. "I woke up and saw Julia's face on the pillow. She looked frightened or in pain."

"Father thinks Trudy probably had a nightmare," Sylvia explained, clutching her silk robe tightly.

"I was awake! I'm sure of it!" Trudy protested. Yet she could understand why they would find her story hard to believe.

"Father is taking a look around the room now," Sylvia said.

At that moment a puzzled-looking Benson Steiburn came back to join them. His first words were directed to Trudy. "It's all right, my girl," he said, then fingered his beard as he searched for the words with which to continue. "You had a right to be frightened. Someone played a macabre trick on you."

"What do you mean?" the young doctor asked.

Steiburn sighed. "I think I should show you what upset Trudy so."

They followed him into the bedroom, and Trudy felt her heart begin to pound again. But she forced herself to move up to the bed, with Sylvia and Carl on either side of her.

Steiburn lifted something from the pillow. "Julia's death mask," he said, holding it so they could all see it. "I had it made at the local undertaker's by a young sculptor who has done some other work for me."

"How did it get here?" Sylvia wanted to know.

"It was removed, obviously, from the desk drawer in the library where I'd placed it for safekeeping. I hadn't quite decided what to do with it. In fact, I was waiting to discuss the matter with Miss Stone—to ask if she wanted a sculpture of her late aunt."

Trudy gasped. "What a fool I've been!"

"Not at all," Benson Steiburn replied. "It's a grisly object, and finding it under such unexpected circumstances was bound to shock you. That is clearly why it was placed there.''

Carl's handsome face showed anger. ''Someone went to the trouble of taking the mask to perpetrate this miserable trick.''

''Someone in this house,'' Sylvia added quietly, looking from one to the other.

''Not necessarily,'' Carl said. ''It could've been someone who had a means of entry into the castle and of getting into this room.''

''There are many entrances to the castle,'' Steiburn admitted grimly. ''We try to see that all are locked, but in a place this large, an entrance door could be over-looked.''

''So whoever decided to do this would have had lit-tle difficulty,'' Sylvia remarked. ''Beyond having to know about the death mask and where it was.''

Her father tugged at his beard again and, with some embarrassment, admitted, ''I've made no secret of the existence of the mask. In fact I've shown it to almost everyone who has visited the house. I was going to show it to Trudy in a day or so.''

She sighed. ''I'm sorry to have woken everyone up and caused all this fuss.''

''You have nothing to reproach yourself for,'' Stei-burn told her. ''As your host, I feel guilty for not af-fording you better protection. I do the best I can, but apparently it's not enough.''

''No one would expect a thing like this to happen. Whoever did it must have a very sick mind.''

''I agree,'' Carl said. ''And I must confess, we have more than our share of neurotics in this small com-munity.''

"Don't frighten her," Sylvia chided him.

"Better to know the truth," he said.

"But why would anyone do such a dastardly thing?" Benson Steiburn murmured, looking at the death mask in his hands.

"Someone wanted to scare her," Carl said. "Perhaps frighten her away for some reason. Someone with an eye on the estate."

Sylvia shook her head. "I think it's even worse than that. I think it's the first move of someone who may try to destroy Trudy."

"But why?" Trudy asked in despair.

"Money," Sylvia said firmly. "You haven't been fully informed by Pascal yet, but you are surely an heiress to a considerable sum."

"I don't think we should jump to conclusions," her father said quickly, "or take the matter too seriously. It might only have been a practical joke on someone's part—but not a funny one! I say we should return to our beds and forget it happened."

Trudy ran a hand through her blond hair. "I don't think I'll sleep again tonight."

"Yes, you will," Sylvia assured her. "I'm taking you to my room. There's an extra bed, and you'll be quite safe."

"That's not necessary," Trudy protested.

Carl gave her a knowing look. "Do as Sylvia says," he told her. "It will give you a chance to recover from the shock. Tomorrow you can return to your own room."

"Excellent idea," Sylvia's father agreed.

And so Trudy found herself joining Sylvia in her large bedroom at the other end of the corridor. Despite the frightening experience she'd had, she fell asleep almost immediately.

IN THE MORNING Sylvia ordered breakfast served in the bedroom. While they were waiting, Trudy went to the window and looked out in time to see Carl get into a town car and drive away. She went to join Sylvia, who was seated at a small round table. The breakfast tray had just arrived.

"Carl just left. He said he had business to do in Lerici."

"My father has interests there," Sylvia said. She looked especially pretty this morning. "He often has Carl handle things for him."

"He's an interesting person—Carl, I mean." Trudy took a sip of orange juice. "But I'm not sure I understand him."

Sylvia laughed. "He's not all that complex!"

"Your father must rely on him a great deal."

"He trusts him completely," the dark-haired woman said, pouring coffee into their cups. "There are many art purchases and other transactions that Carl takes care of entirely on his own."

"A tempting situation, when you think of the large amounts of money involved."

Sylvia nodded. "He has proved himself over the years. He's also a very good doctor. Under his strict guidance and medication, my father's heart condition has improved immensely."

"Every now and then I forget he is a doctor," Trudy said.

"I know what you mean. But this way he can enjoy the life of a millionaire without actually having the responsibilities of one. Few doctors could ever afford the life-style we have here at the castle."

"That's probably why he's so content with his situation," Trudy said. She was still bothered by his having lied to her, despite her interest in him. And while she didn't care to admit it, her view of him was marred. She felt she could no longer count on his sincerity.

Sylvia must have noticed the shadowed expression on her face, for she said quickly, "You're not thinking about that nasty business of the mask again, are you?"

Trudy managed a forlorn smile. "I'm trying hard to forget it."

"And I've brought it up. Clumsy me!"

"I'm over the shock of discovering it."

"I hope so," Sylvia said indignantly. "It was a mean trick, and you can be sure my father will try to find out who was responsible."

"I'm being quite a problem to you," Trudy apologized.

"Nonsense!" Sylvia filled her cup with more coffee. She hesitated, then said, "There is one thing that is bothering me, though."

"Oh?" Trudy's lovely blue eyes showed interest.

Sylvia stared at her for a moment before looking down at her coffee cup. "I'm afraid I wasn't quite frank with you last night."

"Frank about what?"

"We talked about Carl."

"Yes," Trudy said apprehensively. What bothersome fact was Sylvia about to reveal concerning the doctor?

Sylvia hesitated again. "I told you last night that Carl and I were never engaged."

"Yes, you did."

"We weren't, actually," she went on. "But he might have thought we were. We had an understanding. Father wanted us to marry, but I didn't consider it binding."

Trudy listened, amazed and delighted. "Then you were *sort of* engaged?"

"I suppose so. There was no ring or anything like that, no date set. But we did have an understanding. Then I met the man I fell head over heels in love with and later married, and neither Carl nor anything else seemed important."

Trudy listened and wondered. "So you weren't telling the truth when you said you weren't ever engaged?"

"It's the truth as I feel it." Sylvia gave a sad smile. "Perhaps I was trying to make myself seem less spoiled and selfish. The truth is, I met another man and I jilted Carl."

"Thanks for explaining this to me," Trudy said. "What you told me last night was confusing."

"I know. I worried about it."

"Don't think about it again." She smiled broadly, wondering if Sylvia had any idea what a burden she'd lifted from her mind. Trudy looked at her watch. "I'd better go get dressed if I'm to be on time for tennis with Adrian."

"Do you feel up to it?"

"Yes," she said. "I feel much better now." And she did, but for reasons she couldn't confide to the other woman.

"Be careful of that lecherous Italian!" Sylvia teased as she went out.

In her room, she quickly donned the tennis whites Sylvia had let her have. She scarcely thought about the events of the night before, so pleased was she to know that it was Sylvia who had twisted the truth, not Carl.

Adrian, looking very fit in his tennis clothes, glanced at his wristwatch as she joined him downstairs. "I'm glad you're on time. After we finish, I have to go directly to a doubles game on another estate."

"We can cancel our game, if you like," she suggested.

"No," he said, taking her arm and leading her out the front door to his car. "I don't want to do that. But I'll have to leave as soon as we're through playing."

"That's perfectly all right."

He glanced at her, a grim expression on his face. "Before we play, I want to talk to you for a few minutes—give you a warning."

At once she was on the alert. Had he somehow learned about the unpleasant incident of the previous night, or was he concerned about something else?

"What do you want to tell me?" she asked.

They had almost reached the tennis courts, and he delayed his reply until after they'd left the car and were inside the fenced-in area. Then he sat with her on a bench and said, "I think you are in trouble."

Trudy's eyes widened. "Why do you say that?"

He sighed. "Pascal should have been here to meet you and protect you. But you can't depend on him. He was always letting Julia down."

"She kept him on as her lawyer, though," Trudy argued.

"Because she put off finding another," Adrian said in his sour way. "You must know that Steiburn wants to tear the villa down and build an art museum as a monument to himself."

"Yes, I've heard that's what he'd like to do."

"What about Redman, our handsome doctor?" Adrian's tone was spiteful. "What do you make of him?"

"He's been very kind to me," Trudy said, flushing a little.

Romitelli laughed harshly. "You didn't have to tell me that. I was sure he would make himself especially charming for your benefit."

Somewhat put off by that remark, she asserted, "I definitely appreciate what he's done so far."

"You do not understand," the man insisted, grimacing. "What you see is not what he is. He is a very slick customer, our friend Redman."

Trudy stared at him. "I don't think you should say things like that unless you can prove them."

"His deals for Steiburn, who trusts him completely—many of them make money for the doctor. I have heard that in some cases he takes a special payment—a commission—from certain art dealers in return for buying from them."

"That is a very serious accusation," she said sternly. "I'm not interested in hearing any of this unless you have definite proof!"

Adrian smiled sourly. "I see he has taken you in. That is not surprising, as he is a charming scoundrel.

But there is one thing I can tell you that I know for certain."

"What?"

"Though he was more than twenty-five years younger than your aunt, he begged her to marry him. He wanted her money. And she could not see through him, either."

Trudy tried to hide her chagrin. "Then why didn't they marry?"

"Julia had the good sense to turn him down eventually. This was after Sylvia got wise and married someone else. She didn't want to be married for her money, either."

"But Aunt Julia and Carl were good friends," Trudy protested.

"She still believed he was sincere, even though I warned her against him. But she realized that such a marriage would be a mistake."

"How do you know that?"

He raised his eyebrows and shrugged. "How else? She told me, of course."

"So I have only your word for all this."

"A Romitelli does not lie," he declared indignantly. "And now that the good doctor is making himself charming to you, I urge you to watch out. A proposal will not be long in coming."

She was blushing but could not help it. She remembered the words she and Carl had exchanged in the garden. But she did not believe that all he was interested in was the money. Nor did she believe that he had ever asked her aunt to marry him. She had accepted what Sylvia had said about him as the truth, and had

worried a great deal because of it, only to discover
later that it was Sylvia who had not been truthful.

She rose from the bench. "One hears many stories.
I have been told you borrowed large sums of money
from my aunt and refused to pay her back."

He jumped up. "Who told you such a thing?"

"I can't remember," she said. "It doesn't matter."

"It is not true!" he stormed. "Julia paid me certain monies for my company. I was always at her side
when she was lonely and needed someone. There was
never a question of repayment."

Trudy smiled ruefully. "Well, there you are. You
can see how the truth is so often twisted. I think we
should stop this talk and play tennis, especially since
your time is limited."

Adrian slid the cover off his racket, grumbling, "I
am only trying to be a friend to you as I was to Julia."

As Trudy took her place opposite him on the court,
she found herself grateful for the sunshine, since the
morning air was still cool. She made a mental note not
to be talked into playing tennis with Adrian Romitelli
again. She had not liked his conversation, nor did she
care for him.

They volleyed for a few minutes, after which she
knew immediately that, because of his superior skill
and strength, she would be no match for him. But she
carried on as well as she could, noting the look of
smug satisfaction that crossed his face every time he
bested her.

"You may serve first," he said. But her serve was
not swift enough to bother him. He returned it in a

second, and she struggled to get the ball back. She managed once, but the next time it eluded her.

The game went by quickly, since it was so one-sided. Trudy was able to score a few points. Romitelli, far from being a generous opponent, refused to congratulate her whenever she made one of her rare good returns.

Trudy liked the game, so she continued to ignore the personality conflict between them. But the ending was inevitable; he won every game.

Finally he looked at his watch and told her, "I can't give you a chance to balance things. I'm overdue for my other game."

"Please go ahead," she said.

"I can drop you off at the castle," he suggested.

"No, thanks. It's only a short distance, and I'd prefer to walk."

"We'll play another day," he promised. Then he hurried off to his car and drove away.

She watched him go, her mind filled with speculations. She had no intention of playing tennis with him again, certainly not in a singles match. Possibly with a partner like Carl, she might be able to make a good showing against Adrian and whomever he chose for his side of the net.

She put the cover on her racket and let herself out of the fenced-in area. As she was about to start back to the castle, she almost bumped into a brown-haired young man standing there with a big smile on his face. He was wearing white trousers, a white shirt open at the neck and a yellow cardigan sweater.

"You're a spunky little gal!" he exclaimed. His accent was unmistakably American, probably from the

New York area. "You played a courageous game against Romitelli. But he's a lot stronger and more experienced. Still, you bested him at least a couple of times."

"You must have been watching the whole time! But I don't know who you are," she said, stating the obvious in her surprise.

"Don't be frightened," he said jovially. "I'm a Yank like you. My name is Tom Clarendon, and I'm a newspaperman from New York City. Right now I'm here writing a book."

"I see," she said vaguely, not really seeing at all.

He laughed. "I know who you are. You're Julia's niece, Trudy Stone. And you've come here to claim your legacy. Please accept my sympathy to you for your loss."

Trudy was more puzzled now. "How do you know all this?"

"I told you, I'm writing a book—a biography of the actress Lena Morel. And I'm living in her cottage—not, I hasten to add, living with her. It's strictly a business arrangement. I'm turning over half the proceeds of the book to her when it's sold."

Things were clearer to Trudy now. "I understand Lena Morel was a friend of my aunt's," she said.

"That's right, and she was with her the very night she met her death." Tom Clarendon paused for a moment and then said, "I hear you're staying at the castle."

"Yes, I am."

"Lena will be over to see you. You'll like her. She was one of the big names in films once, but now she's lucky to get an occasional part in a B picture over here. That's why she moved to Italy.''

"Really? Are things going that badly with her?"

"The last few years have been rough," Tom said soberly. "And you've probably heard that she drinks too much."

"Yes, I have. Is it true?"

"She's not as bad as people make out. But she does drink more than she should. She was drinking the night Julia drowned in the pool. Lena doesn't say much to anyone else, but I know she partly blames herself for the accident. She still has a certain beauty, and it's a pity what she's doing to herself."

Trudy gave him a knowing look. "There seem to be a number of self-destructive people around here."

"Ah, you've noticed that."

She nodded. "Well, I really must be getting back to the castle now."

"I'll walk you there," he offered.

"There's no need for you to do that," she said.

"The walk will be good for me," he told her.

As they began to stroll along the wooded road, Trudy thought about her unexpected encounter with Tom Clarendon. So he was living at Lena Morel's cottage and writing a book about her. What he'd said about the fading film star seemed to fit in with what she'd heard so far.

"Where is Pascal?" Tom asked, breaking into Trudy's reverie.

"In Lerici, I believe," she said. "I hope to see him on Monday."

"And meanwhile you're at the castle?"

"Yes."

He gave her a wise smile. "So you've met old Benson, daughter Sylvia and the doctor who is an art expert. A nice twist."

"They've all been very kind to me," Trudy said a bit defensively.

"Lena knows them well. I've been over there a few times myself. I'll bet the doctor's made a play for you by now. He's quite a ladies' man."

"I hadn't realized that," Trudy said faintly.

"I think he expected to marry the lovely Sylvia," Tom went on. "But she jilted him for someone else."

"So I've heard," Trudy didn't want to hear anymore.

As the castle came in sight, he said, "All this must be pretty rough on you. If there's anything I can do, please let me know."

"Thanks very much," she said, genuinely grateful for his offer.

He smiled at her. "If you can't help a fellow American, what good are you?"

She laughed. "It's nice to know you're here—not only a fellow American, but a fellow New Yorker, too!"

"And I also play tennis, but not as well or as aggressively as our friend Romitelli. I hope we'll have a game soon."

She nodded. "I'd like that very much."

He studied her closely for a moment. "I think you're a lot like your aunt—as open and friendly as Julia was. She was a wonderful woman. I still can't figure out what really happened that night."

"I'm puzzled about it, too," Trudy said.

"Whenever I try to talk more to Lena about it, she threatens to have hysterics, so I've learned only bits and pieces from her."

"Maybe she'd talk to me," Trudy suggested.

"Don't count on it," Tom said. He glanced around and realized they had reached the castle grounds. He looked over to where Lena Morel's cottage was situated and sighed. "She's waiting for me," he told Trudy. "I guess this is as far as I can go."

Trudy held out her hand. "Thanks for the company and the information."

"Call on me if you need anything," he said, squeezing her hand for a long moment.

"I will, and I'll expect to see you and Miss Morel soon."

"Yes," he said. Then he turned his gaze to the swimming pool by the villa. "By the way, I'd keep away from that pool if I were you."

Slightly startled by his solemn tone, she replied, "Because of what happened, it doesn't have much appeal for me."

"Good." He paused, and then he spoke again. "Have you heard about the ghost of the masked swordsman?"

She smiled grimly. "It's difficult to be at Castle Malice and not be told about it."

He frowned. "Lena might have been drunk that night. And maybe she's even a little mad these days. But there's something you should know. Lena swears that when she went out to the pool and found your aunt's body, the ghost of the masked swordsman was standing back from the pool, watching the body. When he saw Lena, he turned and ran off into the darkness."

CHAPTER FOUR

FOR A MOMENT his words sent a thrill of fear through Trudy. Then she took a firm hold of her emotions and faced him with a calm she did not truly feel. "But then, by all accounts, Lena had been drinking and was in a hysterical state. She might have thought she'd seen anything. And the legend of the masked swordsman seems to be on everyone's lips."

The young newspaperman shrugged. "Still, in this case I think I believe her."

"Even you have become impressed by the ghost!"

"I find the entire place fascinating. Did you know there's a tunnel linking the castle with the villa?"

"No," she said. "No one mentioned it."

"I heard about it from Lena, and it was your aunt who told her about it."

"Did you find out where the tunnel begins and ends?"

"It begins at Castle Malice. Near the entrance to the library there's a door that looks like a closet door, but it leads down to a long underground passage that brings you out into the living room of the villa."

They chatted for a few more moments. Then Tom walked back to the cottage, and Trudy went on to Castle Malice. She was glad she'd met him, for she felt almost as comfortable with him as she did with Carl.

His information about the castle greatly interested her, and she hoped she would soon have the opportunity to see him again.

When she reached the house, neither Sylvia nor her father was in sight. Only the servants were around. She had seen Carl leave for Lerici and did not know when he'd be back. So she went directly up to her room, took a shower and changed into a light blue cotton-knit dress that was flattering to her blond good looks.

Then she went downstairs again and made a deliberate search for the door that Tom had mentioned. She located it without difficulty. Having prepared herself with a flashlight, she decided to explore this approach to the villa she'd inherited. As a precaution, she left the door open behind her as she descended the shadowed stairway. The dampness assailed her nostrils, and she had to dodge the cobwebs that hung from the overhead beams. No doubt the passageway had been used in the old days as a suitable escape route from either of the two buildings in the event of a crisis.

Trudy shivered a little from the cold air, and the beam of her flashlight caught the moisture running down the ancient brick walls. The ground under her feet had been pounded hard by the tread of others for many years. It was a truly eerie spot, and she moved along slowly. Suddenly there was a scurry and a squeal up ahead as a rat bounded out of a hiding place, ran toward her and was lost to sight again.

All Trudy's instincts told her to go back, but her tremendous curiosity about the villa made her press forward. The tunnel narrowed and grew less high, and soon she came to a rusted metal door barred by a latch. She hesitated before it, then tugged at the latch, which gradually creaked free and permitted her to swing the door back and stare into the darkness beyond.

The underground corridor continued much as before. She went on until she came to another door, exactly like the one she had just opened. But when she tried the latch, it would not budge. It was either locked, or jammed in some way. She could go no farther. As she was making a last effort to dislodge it, she heard a sound behind her, a high-pitched mocking laugh that echoed along the musty, shadowy length of the tunnel. She stood motionless with fear for a long moment. When the sound of laughter was not repeated, she decided that some random noise from the outside had accidentally penetrated this place.

Feeling frustrated at not being able to go any farther, Trudy turned and began the journey back. She was more nervous than before and ready to allow any unexpected sight or sound to upset her easily. All at once, she reached the first metal door. At the sight of it, she halted abruptly. It was closed now! But she knew she had left it open behind her, just as she'd done with the door near the library entrance. She fixed the beam of the flashlight on the latch and tried to lift it. This time it would not budge.

"No!" she cried aloud in despair and worked harder at the latch. Her efforts were useless. The door had swung closed, or else someone had deliberately shut it; either way, it was jammed just like the second metal door.

The desperation of her predicament rushed through her mind. She was a prisoner in the short section of tunnel between the two iron doors. She could be there for hours, days—even longer—without being found. A servant could come along, see the door by the library open, and close it, effectively ending any hope Trudy might have of being located and rescued. One day her skeleton would be found there, her clothing in rags, her flesh long ago nibbled away by the rats that infested the place.

This terrifying prospect made her lose all remnants of calm. She began to kick at the heavy iron door and scream at the same time. She kept this up until she was breathless and exhausted; then she slumped against the tunnel wall. Gradually, her strength returned, and again she assailed the unyielding door, shouting until her voice was hoarse. She was in the midst of what she felt might be her last assault when she heard a sound from the other side. A moment later the door swung slowly open.

Benson Steiburn stood there gazing short-sightedly into the darkness, a lantern held high in his right hand. Upon seeing her, he gasped, "Trudy! I can't believe it!"

She stumbled forward, sobbing. "I thought I would never see anyone again—that I was going to die down here!"

"And so you might well have! By some good fortune, I found the upstairs door open, and since it is never used, I thought perhaps you were venturing down here. I prepared myself with a lantern and came to see if indeed you were here and in trouble."

"I was!" she wept. "I was! I should never have come down without checking with you first."

"That is so," he said, putting his arm around her trembling shoulders. "You're perfectly safe now."

"I left this door open, but someone shut it."

"It could have closed by itself," he told her. "We have had that happen before. That is why we never use this tunnel. It's dangerous, and no one should try to get to the villa through it. Or vice versa."

"I heard a mocking laugh behind me," she said, wiping away her tears with her hand. "I don't know if there was anyone here or not."

"I'll wager there wasn't," he said kindly. "And I'm more than delighted to have been able to rescue you. Let's go upstairs for a glass of sherry."

He escorted her to the first floor, then led her out to the rear gardens, where he seated her on an ornamental white chair beneath the palm trees and amid the beds of roses and other flowers. After seeing that she was comfortable, he went back into the house. The sun shone down on her, and she had never been more grateful for its warming light. The experience in the tunnel loomed behind her like a nightmare.

Steiburn returned with two glasses of sherry and sat with her. "Drink it down, my dear. It will do you good."

She sipped the excellent wine. Her throat soon felt relieved from its rawness. "You must be totally out of patience with me," she apologized.

"Not at all," he said. "I find your presence here delightful, as does Sylvia. But you must be more wary, show some caution in these old houses. They are not as innocent as they appear."

"I'm finding that out," she replied with a bleak smile. "It takes such a short time to move from elation to despair."

"You mustn't dwell on it," Steiburn said. "We want you to enjoy yourself here. Indeed, Sylvia is in the village now precisely to see to that."

"What do you mean?"

"She is planning to have a party—in your honor, of course. Everyone will attend, including—we hope—your aunt's attorney, Giuseppe Pascal."

"I'm beginning to have doubts of ever seeing him," Trudy confessed.

"A party will surely bring him back from Lerici. And then you will meet him. I don't suppose you've been told a great deal about your legacy."

"Just that to all intents and purposes I am my aunt's only heir."

"Then expect a great deal of money," Steiburn said. "Julia was left a fortune by her late husband. I think she spent very little of it, so most of it will come your way."

"I'm not sure I care anymore. I think there's something sinister about the villa and the bequest."

The elderly millionaire smiled bleakly. "You have already learned the important lesson that money alone does not necessarily bring happiness."

"But you and Sylvia are happy, aren't you?"

"We might be just as happy in less affluent circumstances," he replied. "It would depend on us."

"I know I shouldn't be imposing on you here, but I'm truly glad I've met you."

"You will stay as long as you like. We want you to feel welcome."

Her head started to ache, so she told him, "If you don't mind, I'd like to go to my room and rest before dinner."

"By all means," he said, rising. "Dr. Redman will return from Lerici in time for the evening meal. And when my daughter comes back from the village, I'll send her up to check on you."

She thanked him and went inside. As soon as she was in her room, she slipped off her dress, scrubbed her hands, which were grimy from her efforts to free herself in the tunnel, and splashed some cold water on her face. Then she stretched out on the bed and almost at once fell into a deep sleep. The tennis game and the ordeal underground had drained her.

When she awakened, she found the pretty, dark-haired Sylvia sitting by her bed and smiling at her. "I'm sorry," Sylvia said. "I disturbed you from a sound sleep."

Trudy propped herself up on one elbow. "It's time I woke up."

"Father told me what happened in the tunnel," the other woman said with awe. "It wasn't bad enough you had to play tennis with Adrian, but you had that dreadful experience, as well."

"It hasn't been entirely my day," Trudy admitted. "I also met someone, a newspaper man."

Sylvia's dark eyes brightened. "I know who! Tom Clarendon!"

"You're right," Trudy said. "How did you guess?"

Sylvia fluttered her hand prettily. "He's the only newspaper chap in the area."

"I'd forgotten what a small world we have here. He introduced himself and told me he's living at Lena Morel's place and writing her biography."

Sylvia grimaced. "I'll bet he doesn't put *all* in print. Between films, she's managed to live a fairly scandalous personal life. And now they say she's having trouble getting work and that her money is running out."

"Tom hinted at the same thing. I guess she gets an occasional Italian film, and she hopes to make some money on the biography."

"Then it will *have* to be scandalous. But she probably won't mind as long as she gets some money from it."

"Tom seemed nice, if a little cynical," Trudy said.

"That's because of his profession. And living with Lena Morel would make anyone cynical. She can be very difficult."

"So I gather, but she can't be worse than Adrian. He was determined to beat me at tennis. Then Tom came along to cheer me up."

"Did Adrian take any time off to gossip? He usually does."

"Just a little. He said he has grave doubts about Carl's honesty and warned me against him."

Sylvia laughed. "I'd expect that. He wants you for himself."

"No chance!"

"You'll be meeting them all again tomorrow night," Sylvia promised. "I'm giving a party for you. Everyone will come. I've been in touch with most of them already, and I'll call the others tonight.''

"There was no need for that,'' Trudy protested.

"I wanted to do it,'' Sylvia insisted. "I love having parties, and I'll be returning to New York soon. I want to do this for you before I leave.''

"I hate to think of you going,'' Trudy said frankly. "I'll feel more alone than ever.''

"Perhaps Pascal will finally show up and settle things. Then you'll be able to return to New York also. What fun for us to meet there!''

Their conversation ended on this happy note. By the time Trudy had put on a green linen dress and gone downstairs, Carl Redman had returned. He was in the living room with Benson Steiburn and Sylvia, the three of them having cocktails.

"You must join us,'' Carl said and went to the bar to prepare a drink for her.

Steiburn beamed at her. "You look especially lovely in that dress, Trudy. That's what's so wonderful about blondes—you can underdress and still look spectacular.''

"Thank you,'' she said.

Sylvia made a face. "You two are dreadful! You make me feel like a frump!''

Her father chuckled and touched his lips to her cheek. "Not in that designer's multilayered yellow chiffon,'' he told her. "And I know what a fortune it cost.''

Sylvia linked her arm in his. "Just as long as you think we're *both* beauties.''

"I do,'' he assured her.

Carl handed Trudy her drink. "What have you been up to all day?"

Her eyes widened. "You mean you haven't heard yet?"

"I'm afraid not. I've only been back for a few minutes."

She quickly told him, ending with, "I think that's rather good for one day."

He frowned slightly. "You shouldn't have gone into that tunnel alone. It's not safe to use any longer. You could have died down there."

"I know," she said. "Happily, my luck lasted and Mr. Steiburn found me."

"I'm going to have that door by the library sealed," Carl promised her. "It will be a priority project."

Steiburn nodded his approval.

They finished their drinks and went in to dinner. Sylvia immediately launched into a discussion of the party.

"We'll have it in the rear gardens," she said. "I've hired the three-piece band from the village." To Trudy, she added, "The trio is very good, and the man from the village inn is coming with his staff to take care of all the food. He's a genius at it. We've had the same team before, and the food was marvelous."

Benson Steiburn nodded. "My last birthday was a feast. My son-in-law was here then. He and Sylvia made a lovely couple when they led the dancing."

Sylvia gave Carl a challenging glance. "You shall lead me this time."

He laughed easily. "I'll gladly be your partner. So will all the other males. I've never known you to be a wallflower."

"And maybe that clever rascal of a lawyer will attend," Steiburn said.

Sylvia nodded. "Pascal has promised to be here." She turned to Trudy. "I caught him at his Genoa office today, just after I spoke to you in your room. He asked that I apologize to you for him."

"I'm looking forward to our meeting," Trudy said.

Sylvia went on excitedly about the party all through the meal, and Trudy could see that social events meant a lot to her. She also thought that Sylvia was paying a great deal of attention to Carl, which made her wonder if Sylvia was still in love with him. She felt she was in a strange little corner of the world, in which hardly anyone meant what he said or did. She doubted she could ever be a part of it.

When Sylvia and her father left the table after dinner, Carl pulled out Trudy's chair for her and asked, "A penny for your thoughts?"

"I'm telling myself this is a world that's strange to me, not at all what I've been used to."

"Is that so bad?"

"Yes and no," she said with a small smile. "I'd rather drop the subject."

"A stroll in the gardens?" he suggested.

"It should be lovely out there," she said.

He led her through a marble-floored, plant-lined room and out a pair of French doors to the rear patio. When they were outside, he pointed up at the overhanging tree branches. "Tomorrow night it will be a wonder world of bright lights and music. Sylvia has dozens of colorful magic lanterns that she hangs in the entire area."

"Did my aunt come here often?" she asked as they continued on in the moonlit garden.

"Quite often," he said. "At least until Lena Morel came here to live. I always felt she had a bad influence on Julia. She kept her over at her own place, drinking. It wasn't good for her."

"That could have led to her death," Trudy said soberly.

"It's possible," he agreed.

"Did you and Julia ever quarrel?"

There was an almost imperceptible hesitation on Carl's part before he laughed nervously and said, "Never! What gave you that idea?"

"I just wondered. You knew her a long time. I hear she was usually good-natured but that she could be difficult at times."

"That's a fairly accurate description of her," he agreed.

"Were you in love with her?" she asked, watching him closely.

His handsome face showed surprise. "Julia was a good many years older than I."

"That doesn't answer my question."

He spread his hands. "I was fond of her, yes. But to say I was in love with her is preposterous."

"Would you have married her if she had encouraged you?"

Carl looked more amazed than before. "Why on earth are you asking me all these crazy questions?"

She smiled a secret smile. "I have my reasons."

He frowned and then suddenly exclaimed, "Romitelli!"

"What about him?"

"He's been telling you tales about me. He's done that before. His story is all a pack of lies. He's the one who wanted to marry Julia. He's desperate for money, you know."

"So you've said."

"And I fully expect him to propose to you," Carl warned her. "No matter how weak you are at tennis. You have money, so he'll forgive that."

Trudy laughed in spite of herself. "You all tell such wild stories about one another. Tom Clarendon should spend his life here writing all your biographies."

Carl's eyebrows raised. "So you've met him, too!"

"This afternoon."

"All the young men in Palina are after you, it seems."

"Our meeting was purely accidental," she maintained.

He looked skeptical. "I wonder."

"I'm sure it was. He felt Adrian was unfair to me on the court."

"He's not a bad fellow," Carl said grudgingly. "But to me, his being with Lena Morel so much is a mark against him."

"It's his job. He's doing her life story."

"That will make some reading!"

"I was glad to meet him." She sighed. "It was the only nice thing that happened to me today."

"Really?"

"You know how it's been. That death mask on my pillow last night, and then being trapped in that awful old tunnel today."

"Sorry," he said, more gently. "You know I do care what happens to you."

"You said that last night."

"And I meant it," he promised her, halting along the path through the trees. They were a distance from the house now, although its lights could still be seen.

She gave him a serious look. "If you knew how much I want to believe that."

Carl took her into his arms and said, "You must trust me."

"I want to," she said unhappily. "I really do. But I hear so many stories I wind up being confused and frightened."

"My poor darling," he murmured.

Trudy was thrilled to be in his arms again, but then there was a violent interruption to this tender moment they were enjoying. From ahead there came the anguished cry of a person in pain or some kind of distress. The cry sounded again and caused them to break apart and stare into the darkness with alarm.

"It sounds like a human voice," Carl said.

"Yes. But I can't tell whether it's a man or a woman."

"Nor I."

She was holding on to his hand and listening. "It's quiet now. What shall we do?"

He gave a deep sigh. "I should go and look. Someone may be in trouble—attacked by a thug or having a seizure. I can't very well ignore what may be a call for help."

"I'll go with you," she said quickly.

"No. If there's some criminal out there, you'd be in more danger. If there's another explanation, you'd still be better off here."

"You want me to wait here," she said faintly, the echo of those dreadful cries still vivid in her mind.

"Yes."

"I'd rather go with you!"

"Stay right here and don't move! I'll be back for you in a moment or two!" With that he plunged ahead, into an area where the overhanging trees shut out any trace of the moonlight.

Their moment of happiness had been dashed in a matter of minutes. She stood there, miserable and afraid, listening for any sounds from ahead, any hint of what might be happening to Carl.

Now it was all silence. She debated turning and running back to the castle but feared that would be deserting Carl. He had explicitly asked her not to move from this spot. The darkness pressed close to her with menacing hands.

Then, from almost behind her, she heard a soft rustle of branches. She swung around and screamed as she saw the figure of a masked, black-cloaked swordsman hovering incredibly close to her.

CHAPTER FIVE

TRUDY STOOD THERE transfixed, gazing at the phantomlike creature in horror. Then the masked swordsman raised a hand as if making a sign of some sort for her benefit. She tried to scream again, but no sound came from her lips. Everything dissolved around her as she toppled down in a faint.

The next thing she was aware of was Carl bending over her and pleading, "Trudy, it's all right! Believe me, we're quite safe!"

She stared at him with troubled eyes and raised herself up on an elbow. "You saw him?"

"I saw no one. It must have been some animal cry that fooled us. There was absolutely no one there." He took her gently by the arms. "Let me help you to your feet."

She allowed him to assist her and brushed the leaves from her dress. "I don't know about you, but I definitely saw something. That's what made me faint."

He frowned. "Who? What?"

Her smile was rueful. "Surely you can guess."

"The ghost of the masked swordsman?"

"Yes."

"Where?"

"Right there." She pointed to the trees behind her.

"You saw him in this light?"

"Clearly," she insisted, beginning to realize that he was doubting her.

Carl looked unhappy. "I think you had a bad case of nerves. It only takes a little imagination to have a waving branch become a moving figure in this near darkness."

Trudy gave him a look of reproach. "I'd hoped you would believe me."

"I'm only telling you what I think really happened," was his reply. "You've had two bad experiences in the past twenty-four hours, so it's understandable you'd be on edge and conjure up a ghost in this lonely spot."

Pleading showed in her blue eyes. "I *did* see him."

"I hope not," he said wearily. "You know it isn't thought to be good luck to see the swordsman's ghost."

"What do you mean?"

He hedged. "It just is most unfortunate."

"I know what I saw," she insisted a trifle petulantly. She had never believed the charming Carl could be so obtuse. "I demand that you tell me."

His face shadowed. "It will only make you more nervous."

"I'm not a child," she said firmly. "Please don't treat me like one."

Carl stared at her for a long moment before he said, "Well, you've asked for it. The legend is that whoever sees the phantom figure dies a violent death shortly after."

His words had more impact on Trudy than she'd expected. She stared at him and gasped, "They say Aunt Julia was visited by the ghost before her death!"

Carl sighed. "It's all ignorant superstition. You are too intelligent to be swayed by it. You're badly upset, and that's the only reason I didn't want to tell you. Ordinarily, you would laugh at the story."

"I'm not laughing now," she said quietly. "Let's go back to the house."

As they walked back toward the castle along the wooded path, he linked his arm in hers and told her, "I'm going to give you a sedative to take before you go to bed. You're in need of an unbroken night's sleep."

"Is that your answer to the phantom? To drug me?"

"You mustn't consider it that way," he said quickly. "I'm thinking entirely of your health."

"Thank you," she replied in a slightly mocking tone. She still resented his refusal to believe her.

"About your seeing the swordsman," Carl went on rather urgently. "I suggest you don't mention it to the others at all."

Trudy gave him a side glance. "Are you afraid they will believe me?"

"No. Again, I'm trying to protect you. Wild stories are apt to weaken their belief in you. It could be that if something more potentially dangerous turned up, they wouldn't listen to you."

"As you refuse to now."

He halted and turned to her. "Accept my judgment in this, please," he urged. "I have my reasons, which I'll explain later."

Trudy stared at him and could not believe his earnest face reflected a lie. She must at least give him marks for being sincere. If he asked for her silence for a little while, it might be wise to listen to him.

"All right, I'll say nothing. But on one condition."

"What is that?"

"Later, you'll examine the area around where I stood and see if you can find any clue that might indicate if someone was playing the ghost."

To her pleased surprise, he showed no resistance to this request. "I'll be quite willing to do that. And if I come upon anything suspicious, I will follow it up and let you know."

She managed a small smile. "Thanks. Then we have an agreement."

"I'll be glad when Pascal arrives," the doctor said as they resumed walking. "He should be here taking care of you and your interests."

"I imagine he has many other clients."

"None more important than you. He'll be at the party and will no doubt remain in his office in Lerici for a series of discussions with you."

"I understood his office was in Genoa."

"That's his main office," Carl said. "He has a small one in Lerici, where his father was born and first practiced law. The elder Pascal has been dead a couple of years, and Giuseppe has neglected the business since then, allowing his late father's associates to do whatever has to be done."

They reached the castle and made their way to the living room. Steiburn and Sylvia were still there, but now they had guests. Tom Clarendon stood up to give Trudy a smiling greeting. A languid-looking woman with short, fuzzy brown hair and beringed fingers sat sprawled in a high-backed chair, smoking a cigarette in a long holder.

"This is Julia's niece, Trudy Stone," Steiburn told the woman. "You recall Julia spoke of her. Trudy, this is Lena Morel."

Lena eyed Trudy without much interest. "You are the niece who lives in New York."

"Yes," Trudy said politely. "May I say I look forward to seeing you in your future films."

The faded beauty raised her heavy lids. "You actually have manners! How unusual to find them among the young these days."

"Is that a blanket indictment of us all?" Sylvia asked with some humor, undoubtedly trying to lighten any offense from Lena's remark.

"You and your father have spent so much time over here, you are almost Europeans," Lena said in her slightly accented but pleasant voice. "And Carl is well on his way to becoming a token member of our group."

There was a twinkle in Carl's eyes as he said, "What about Adrian Romitelli?"

"That one!" Lena dismissed him with a wave of her cigarette holder. "He would be a disgrace to any continent. He is no example."

Everyone laughed at this. The little group then divided up, and Trudy made it a point to take a chair beside the one in which Lena was seated. The others drifted over to the bar on the opposite side of the room.

Trudy wanted to make the most of this small moment of privacy with the aging film star. "I understand you were with Aunt Julia when she died," she said.

The older woman studied Trudy from under her heavy lids, and the gleam in her eyes was not one of warmth. "That was my misfortune."

Trudy was taken by surprise. "I thought you were the best of friends."

"We were. I was truly fond of her. But it was a nasty experience being there when she drowned."

"Naturally I'm interested in the details."

Lena Morel uttered a soft moan. "Please don't ask me a lot of annoying questions."

Trudy saw it wasn't the time for any lengthy discussion of the tragedy. "I have just one question I'd like to ask."

The actress eyed her grimly. "I make no promise to answer it."

Trudy managed a smile. "That's all right. I'll ask it in any case. I've heard that you saw the ghost of the masked swordsman leaving the scene when you came out and found my aunt's body in the swimming pool. Is that true?"

"Yes, it is," Lena Morel said carefully. "Of course, many people do not believe it. They think the phantom doesn't exist. But I know better. I know poor Julia was visited by the black-cloaked ghost, and it was her death warrant."

Trudy decided the woman was at least consistent. This was the story she had told earlier. "Thank you. I won't bother you with any more questions."

"But I shall put a few to you," the actress said acidly.

Trudy thought she could justifiably question Lena Morel's right to do this, but then she decided it might be better to humor her and perhaps find out more information that way.

"What is it you want to know?" she asked politely.

"Have you or your lawyer seen Julia's will yet?"

"No. Pascal sent a brief résumé of it to me in New York. He'll explain the details to me here."

Lena smiled sourly. "Sounds like Giuseppe. He's not the man his father was."

"So I've heard."

"Do you plan to reopen the villa?"

"I don't know," Trudy said. "You see, I haven't been inside it yet. But I have been told it's in poor shape and should probably be torn down."

"Enough money spent on it by a person with the right taste would make it livable again," the actress said. "But you are too young to know or really care."

"I don't know what Julia's plans for it were." Trudy hoped she might get a useful reply from the woman.

Lena Morel lost some of her acid manner as she said, "Julia was reluctant to close the place. She had come to love it. I also adored the villa. We talked about the possibility of seeing to the necessary repairs. She was making plans to do that when she met her death. She even asked me if I would come and live with her. I was seriously thinking about it when the tragedy took place."

"That is interesting," Trudy said. "Benson Steiburn told me he advised her to tear the place down."

Lena's thin face showed a sneer. "Surely you know why?"

Trudy shrugged.

"I'll tell you the only correct one. He wants to build an art museum there as a memorial to himself. His ego surpasses everything. It even outweighed his friendship for your aunt."

"I will have to make my own decision when I tour the place," Trudy said.

"You ought to be living there—now!" Lena snapped.

"Mr. Steiburn was very kind about my coming here. And it would be a big job to find new servants and have the villa officially open."

"Bother that!" the actress exclaimed. "Living there would give you a real feeling for the place, make you truly want it to be your home."

"I hadn't thought of that," Trudy admitted.

"Be sure that Benson has," the older woman warned her. "That is one of his reasons for keeping you here."

"I can't believe that is his chief reason."

"Believe what you like," Lena said, relapsing into her former bitter mood. "So you met Tom today?"

"Yes."

"He told me you were pretty, which didn't surprise me. Don't build on your looks though. They are fleeting. I was a beauty once, and look at me today."

"You still have a great deal," Trudy said politely.

"I am a formidable wreck," the faded screen star declared. "Tom likes you," she said, abruptly changing the subject.

"He seems very nice," Trudy ventured.

"He said he invited you to visit us. Please do. We can go swimming in the ocean, the only decent place to do it."

"That is very kind of you."

"Tom is writing my life story. We hope it will be a bestseller. Perhaps it will even get my career going again."

"I do hope it's a success."

Lena Morel studied her with more approval. "You're really not a bad young woman. But you must be cautious about your company here."

"So I've been told."

"Keep away from that Romitelli. He is poisonous!"

Trudy smiled. "I've discovered that."

Lena's face showed indecision for a few seconds; then she asked, "You were walking in the gardens with Carl?"

A little surprised at the question, Trudy nodded. "Yes. We took a stroll together."

"Do you do it often?"

Her surprise increased. "Have you a reason for asking that?"

"Yes."

"I've enjoyed meeting him," she said frankly. "We have spent some time in each other's company."

Lena glanced across the room to where Carl and Sylvia appeared to be having an intimate conversation. Then she looked at Trudy and said, "You notice how close they are."

Trudy shrugged. "They have been friends for a long while. She doesn't see as much of him since she got married."

"Doesn't she?" Lena Morel asked with sly cynicism. "It strikes me that she returns here a good deal—and most of the time without her husband."

"She is devoted to her father," Trudy said, feeling awkward in her defense of Sylvia. "He is getting old and is alone."

"Is that her story?"

"Isn't it obvious?"

"Has she ever shown any jealousy over your strolls with the handsome doctor?" Lena asked calmly.

The question shocked Trudy. "On the contrary! When I first arrived, Sylvia suggested I should take an interest in him."

Lena nodded. Her smile was icy. "What a clever girl she is."

"Why do you say that?"

"Do you play bridge?"

"No."

"You should learn. Misdirection can be an important part of it."

Before the conversation could continue, Tom came over, looking extremely attractive in a white silk shirt, pale yellow jacket and navy pants. Trudy was forced to admit to herself that in his own way he was as good-looking as Carl. His disposition seemed to be even more pleasant. The two men were very different types, yet their qualities nearly matched; it would be hard to choose between them.

"Time to leave, Lena," he said. "We have a swim date planned for the morning. I want to work on the book after that. And you'll need to rest in the afternoon before the party begins."

The film star rose languidly from her chair and reprimanded Tom. "You have become entirely too protective, young man."

He smiled. "I have to be. I've invested a good deal of time in you, remember?"

Lena showed a wan smile and patted his arm. "At least you care. Now that Julia is gone, I can't think of anyone else who does." And she gathered up her handbag as she prepared to leave.

"I'll see you tomorrow," Tom told Trudy.

"That will be very nice," she agreed.

Lena had taken his arm now and was leaning on it. "Come by the cottage soon. You are always welcome. Julia used to make it her second home. You may do the same."

"I will come by," Trudy promised. "And we must arrange to do some swimming while the ocean is still warm."

Benson Steiburn and Sylvia saw the two guests out, and Trudy found herself alone with Carl once again. The handsome, dark-haired doctor gazed at her with an air of amused tolerance.

"You and Lena had a good old chat," he said.

"She's a character," Trudy agreed. "But she has a stimulating mind."

"How do you like her friend?" Carl asked slyly.

"Her biographer?"

"Yes. I suppose that is his official title. I sometimes wonder if he doesn't have an even closer relationship with her."

"I think they're merely friends."

"Fair enough. He seemed to enjoy talking to you."

"I enjoy his company," she replied.

"I'll be interested in seeing that book, if it ever appears," Carl said, his tone clearly indicating that he would be surprised if it did. "Tom turned up here suddenly a few months ago," he added.

She offered him a knowing smile. "Your little group is not exactly given to welcoming strangers with open arms."

"Can you blame us?" He smiled. "One Romitelli is enough."

"Poor Adrian," she said. Then she looked at Carl very directly. "You won't forget we have an agreement?"

For a moment he appeared puzzled. Then his face cleared and he said, "Of course. I thank you for saying nothing. I will take a good look out there."

Sylvia and her father returned. Good-nights were said, and before Carl left Trudy, he gave her a small bottle of yellow tablets. "Take two. You need the rest."

She did as he'd asked, and within ten minutes of getting into bed, she fell into a deep, dreamless sleep.

When she awoke, it was morning, and the sun was streaming in the windows of her room. It seemed to her as if no time had passed at all. She did feel rested but also slightly giddy-headed. She took a shower cold enough to wake her thoroughly. When she emerged from it, she felt alert and well.

She decided to dress casually today, so put on jeans and a T-shirt. It wasn't until she was ready to leave the room that she noticed something on her bedside table that hadn't been there before—a man's fancy black leather glove with the intricate stitching and design of an earlier day.

As she stared at it, her first frightening thought was of the masked swordsman. She was certain he'd worn such black gloves when she'd had that brief glimpse of him the night before. Then she recalled Carl's promise to go back and search for clues. It seemed clear that he had done that, found the glove and come to leave it with her as she slept.

The presence of the glove brought up a whole new line of possibilities and bolstered her belief that the so-called ghost that had been seen lately was actually someone in disguise, someone using the legend of the swordsman to pursue his own evil actions. And for some reason, she was apparently one of his targets.

She forced herself to pick up the leather glove, then stuffed it into the side pocket of her jeans. She was excited by the find and elated to know that Carl had kept his word to her. Just when she began to doubt him, something invariably happened to give him a clean bill of character.

The only one in the breakfast room was Benson Steiburn. He greeted her with a smile. "You look very rested."

Trudy sat down across from him. "I took some pills and had a good sleep."

"Some of Carl's yellow ones." He nodded. "I've used them many times."

She glanced out the window and saw that it was a pleasant, sunny day. "It should be lovely for the party tonight."

"It means a busy day and night. There will be a lot of people here—some you may not even be able to meet. But I'll make sure you get to know the important ones."

She smiled over her coffee. "I had a long chat with Lena Morel last night."

"I saw that." Steiburn chuckled. "Was she in her usual sour mood?"

"Much of the time."

He looked thoughtful. "I am of the opinion that if Julia had lived, she was going to have Lena join her as a companion. It's getting increasingly more difficult for Lena to make ends meet at the cottage on her own."

"I had the same impression. She seemed to think Aunt Julia might have repaired the villa rather than sell it and that they would have lived there."

"No doubt Lena encouraged that for her own sake, but it would have been a grave mistake for Julia. She'd have been saddled with that old house and Lena, as well. I gave her the best advice when I told her to sell it."

"I can appreciate the conflict, since you wanted the land for your art museum."

Benson Steiburn looked embarrassed. "I'm not saying I wouldn't build there if the land became available. But I could do that in many other locations."

Sylvia came striding in, wearing khaki riding breeches and a khaki shirt open at the neck. She put a hand on Trudy's shoulder and said, "Don't believe him, darling. He can't wait to get his hands on the villa."

"You are joking, Sylvia!" her father said in reprimand. "And you are also embarrassing Trudy as the new owner of the villa."

Sylvia stood with her legs apart and her arms akimbo. "If silly Giuseppe Pascal ever arrives to make it all legal."

"He'll be here tonight," her father said. "And when Trudy sees the villa, she can decide for herself. There will be no pressure from me."

"I never felt there would be," Trudy told him.

"I imagine you gained some idea of its condition from your adventure in the tunnel yesterday," Sylvia said.

"I did," Trudy agreed, not really wanting to discuss it further at this point.

Sylvia smiled at her. "I can see you're dressed to help with the decorating. As soon as you've finished breakfast, come out and join us."

"Where is Carl?"

"Helping me, where else? I'm not climbing any ladders to the tops of those tall trees."

Steiburn frowned. "The handymen should be doing it rather than Carl. He's important to us in this household, and we don't want him to have an accident."

"I promise to take care of him," Sylvia said and left as quickly as she'd arrived.

Trudy followed her out a few minutes later. She was impressed by the amount of decorating that had already been done. Lanterns and streamers hung from many trees in the garden. Fancy cloths covered the tables set out on the grass, and a number of folding chairs were stacked up beside them.

"Hello!

Trudy looked up and saw Carl on one of the wrought-iron balconies, making it look gala with colored streamers. "You're doing well!" she said, waving and laughing.

"I'll be down in a minute."

She waited to see what task Sylvia might have for her. The dark girl was nowhere in sight; only the servants were there, working.

After a few moments Carl came out. "You look better after your rest," he told her.

"What about this?" she asked. "I found it on my bedside table when I woke up." She handed him the black leather glove.

He took it and held it before him, a frown appearing on his face. "I'm afraid I know nothing about it. I've never seen it before."

CHAPTER SIX

TRUDY WAS STARTLED by his words. Still not able to believe what he'd said, she said, "You're telling me you didn't leave this glove in my room?"

"Not only did I not leave it there, I have never seen it before."

"Then where did it come from?"

"Where, indeed?" he repeated grimly. "And why?"

"I was sure you'd gone outside and found it where I'd seen the ghost. I was positive the glove had been dropped there."

"I did go out there, but I found nothing. Not even the bushes were disturbed."

Trudy's lovely face revealed her dismay. "Then this changes the whole situation," she said. "Whoever left it in my room must have done so to scare me. Another evil trick!"

"It's possible," he admitted. "But maybe there's a different explanation for its being there. Let me have it for a little while, and I'll speak to the servants and try to find out if they know anything about it."

"I suppose this will end the usual way, with none of them having anything to tell," she said ruefully. "Even before I look at the villa, someone is trying to frighten me away."

He placed a placating hand on her arm. "Please, try not to think about it. Tonight is your night. Sylvia is doing all this in your honor."

She sighed. "I'm sorry I encouraged her. She shouldn't have bothered."

Carl laughed. "She's having a wonderful time doing it. She loves parties."

At that moment Benson Steiburn appeared. "The Caselli modern you bought in Genoa has finally arrived at the railway station, Carl. The station attendant wants us to pick it up."

"I'll go at once," Carl said.

"No, you won't!" It was Sylvia who protested loudly. "I need you here." Turning to her father, she said, "What is to stop you from going and getting it yourself?"

The older man took the suggestion good-naturedly. "If you can't spare Carl, I'll be happy to do it."

"I need him here all morning."

"I'll go on my own," Steiburn said. Then he looked at Trudy. "What about you? Would you like to come with me and see some more of the countryside?"

"I'm supposed to be helping, as well," she said.

"It's your party, so there's really no need for you to be here," Sylvia told her. "Go along with Father. It will be good for both of you."

A few minutes later, Trudy found herself seated beside Benson Steiburn in the white convertible. Since the weather was warm and sunny, he kept the top down. She tied a scarf over her head as protection against the sun and the wind. The art collector had donned a white peaked cap.

As they drove up the winding road that led to the main highway, he chuckled. "My daughter is most possessive of Carl."

"He doesn't seem to mind."

"They get along well. Once I'd hoped they would marry. But my New York manager came along and turned her head completely."

"She seems to have a happy marriage," Trudy remarked.

"So she says," Sylvia's father allowed. Then he frowned and added, "I wonder, sometimes. She spends so much time over here with me."

Trudy smiled. "Sylvia is a devoted daughter."

He nodded. "I should be pleased. But I feel she should spend at least half the year in New York. She doesn't."

Trudy tried to make the best of a difficult conversation. "You'd be surprised how many married people have that life-style these days."

They had reached the main road, and the drive to the station was brief. Trudy noted that once again the place seemed deserted. The only person there was the stout little attendant, who came running out to place the carefully wrapped painting in the trunk of the convertible. Steiburn thanked him and gave him a generous tip. The little man beamed his pleasure and backed away almost in a reverential bow.

"I'll take you through the village now," Steiburn told Trudy.

Palina proved to be a tiny hamlet nestled on a hillside by the ocean. Its houses were done in a variety of pastel colors and had quaint little shutters of a timeless style. There was a wide beach of gleaming white sand, and as Steiburn drove on, Trudy saw more expensive villas and stately homes on tree-lined streets.

"We'll go by the business area and the flower-and-fruit market," he said. Soon they passed a group of various stalls crowded with many shoppers.

Steiburn said, "The beaches aren't as filled with people now as they were a few weeks ago. The village is also more deserted."

"Is it mostly a tourist area?" she asked.

"Tourists provide a lot of the revenue, but this is good fishing and wine-growing country."

"I think I love the Italian Riviera."

He laughed, then turned around to drive out of the village. "I chose it for my retirement and because it gives me easy access to the great art centers of Europe."

"I didn't spend enough time in Genoa." As she said this, she thought of the gypsy and her peculiar warning. Once again she wondered what the woman had seen in her future and whether it had anything to do with Castle Malice.

"The Genoese know how to spend money to beautify their city. It is full of princely mansions and has at least two important museums. They have a full season of opera there every winter. And would you believe, Genoa has over four hundred churches!"

They were heading back to the castle, and Trudy found herself wishing the drive had been longer. "Thank you for the tour," she said.

"A most limited one, I fear."

"It's good to get away from the castle area, if only for an hour. Not that it isn't lovely," she added quickly.

"I understand," he told her. "I regret the various things that have taken place. Coming after your dear aunt's death, they surely must have bothered you."

She gave him a rueful glance. "I think I now believe in your ghost."

Steiburn nodded. "I can't say that I blame you."

"Someone wants me to sell the villa and leave."

"I'd like to see you sell the villa," he replied. "But that doesn't mean you'd have to leave. You could build a new, smaller place. There's lots of land available."

Trudy's face was shadowed. "I don't think whoever it is wants that. He is trying to frighten me away."

"If you're thinking of the black-masked swordsman, he's impartial. A great many people claim to have seen him."

"The phantom figure is only part of it," Trudy said.

"When Pascal arrives, you will see the villa and decide how you wish to deal with it."

"Yes," she said, then asked him, "Would you tear it down soon?"

"At once. I'm not a young man, and I would like to see the museum built while I'm still alive."

As they rounded a bend, they passed a small, dark sedan. Tom was at the wheel, and Lena sat beside him.

"They will be at the party tonight," Benson Steiburn said.

"I tried to get her to tell me some more details of what happened the night of Julia's drowning. But she wasn't anxious to talk about it."

"Lena is strange but greatly talented. It is sad that the passage of time has ruined her career. She's too old now for the fiery romantic ladies she used to depict on the screen.''

"Have you known her a long time?"

"No. She came to the cottage only a few years ago. Before that she lived mostly in Beverly Hills."

They turned down the same winding road by which they had left and soon came out into the open cliff area that Castle Malice dominated. Once again Trudy experienced a sensation of uneasiness. She was back in this closed-off area where so many mysterious and frightening things had taken place.

Steiburn drove by the pool and said grimly, "No one has used it lately. It might well be filled in."

"It has a brooding look," she admitted. "And everyone knows Aunt Julia died in it. Not to mention the stories about the masked swordsman lurking there."

"We bred him at Castle Malice," Steiburn said with an attempt to lighten their talk. "Blame us for him. I hope the party goes well and that you enjoy the rest of your stay with us." He brought the sleek convertible to a halt by the side door and went off to summon a servant to take care of the painting.

Trudy walked over to the rear gardens. Neither Sylvia nor Carl was in sight, but several of the male servants were still stringing up decorations. The place now had a proper carnival look. And seated glumly in his tennis whites amid it all was Adrian Romitelli.

She came up to him and laughed. "You are early for the party! But welcome!"

The pinch-faced man stood up. "I have not been invited for tonight's affair," he said stiffly, his accent more pronounced now.

Trudy's blue eyes showed sympathy. "I'm sure it's an accident. No one meant to overlook you. I give you my personal invitation."

"I will accept your invitation," he said formally. "Though I believe Sylvia purposely neglected to ask me."

She knew this was all too likely true but felt no impulse to hurt the strange young man. "Let's not worry about it," she said. "You're coming."

"I stopped by to see if you'd care to play some tennis."

"Not today. We're busy decorating. And I want some time to rest."

His eyes were fixed on her. "You resent that I won last time."

"No!" she protested. "I enjoyed playing with you. We'll do it again another day. I can learn a lot being on the court with you."

His expression remained sober. "I am your best person to rely on for anything here. You may not think so, but it is true. If your aunt were alive, she'd tell you that."

Now Trudy was wondering how she was going to get rid of him. "I'm sure that's so," she said vaguely.

"Some people you consider friends are a good deal less than that," he assured her.

She glanced around in desperation. "I wonder where Carl and Sylvia are."

"They went inside when I arrived. I can do without those two."

She smiled and made no answer. Finally she said, "You may as well try to find a game with someone else. It won't do any good to remain here any longer."

"I'll come back tonight, if only to spite them." To her relief, he stalked off.

The moment Adrian had left, the rear door opened, and a laughing Sylvia and Carl came out. Still choked with laughter, Sylvia exclaimed, "I thought you'd never get rid of him!"

"You two!" Trudy said accusingly. "You hurt his feelings."

"Long overdue," Carl told her. "He's insulted everyone in the village. We're just getting our own back."

"We've wasted precious minutes," Sylvia chided them. "Let's finish things up for the party."

That took until after lunch. Then Trudy went up to her room and stretched out on her bed for a nap, which turned into a sound sleep and lasted until late afternoon. As soon as she woke up, she rushed to shower and start to dress. She decided to wear her best party outfit, a crimson strapless dress that provided a striking contrast to her blondness.

When she was ready, she went down the hall to Sylvia's room and knocked on the door. Sylvia opened it, wearing a lovely white gown with short sleeves. The dark-haired girl's eyes widened with admiration on seeing Trudy.

"My! You look better than I've ever seen you!"

"This dress isn't as good as yours or as dignified," Trudy pointed out.

"I found this in a favorite shop in Rome," Sylvia said, studying herself in the long mirror by the door.

"I'm getting excited. How many people will be here?"

"Thirty or forty," Sylvia replied. "Most of the Yanks and Brits in the village, along with a token Italian or two."

Trudy nodded and teased her by saying, "Like Adrian."

"Your guest and your responsibility," Sylvia teased back.

As they chatted, the sound of music wafted up from the gardens; this was their signal to go down below. The trio from the village was playing selections from older American musicals such as *Oklahoma* and *Fiddler on the Roof*, and was much better than Trudy had expected.

Smoking a huge cigar and wearing a white dinner jacket, Benson Steiburn was moving about importantly, making sure that everything was in order. A smiling Carl joined the women a few minutes later, a red carnation in the buttonhole of his well-tailored tuxedo jacket.

He winked at Trudy and said, "Better than hospital duty, don't you think?"

"I'm beginning to understand you, Dr. Redman," she said with mock formality.

They had little chance to say much more before the first guests arrived, a town official and his wife. Trudy was introduced to the rotund couple. Then Lena appeared, wearing a purple gown that made her seem taller. A white fox fur was draped around her shoulders. Tom was with her, looking trim in a dinner jacket.

"Ravishing," Lena complimented Trudy as they greeted each other.

"I can hardly wait to get you in my arms!" Tom exclaimed.

Trudy laughed. "Aren't you rushing things a little?"

"I mean, to dance." He grinned and moved on.

A steady stream of people showed up, and soon the garden area was filled with music and some fairly loud conversation. Adrian Romitelli came alone and insisted on kissing Trudy's hand.

Waiters moved about, passing out food and drink. Small groups formed and then disbanded. Trudy was amazed at the number of well-dressed women and men who had donned their formal best in honor of her. Of course, the host was Benson Steiburn, not Sylvia, and most people catered to the whims of the millionaire. Because the party was in his home, its success could be assured.

She gazed at everyone in awe. So this was the world her aunt Julia had known and of which she herself was soon to be a part. She wasn't at all sure she was ready for it. And there was some unknown enemy who did not want her to take her rightful place in it. The attempts to terrify her had surely been geared to make her turn her back on all this.

At her elbow, Tom said slyly, "My, what serious thoughts we are having."

She turned quickly to look into the newspaperman's face. "I'm not used to this sort of partying."

"Better prepare yourself," he told her. "Entertaining will be expected of you when you open the villa."

"I'm not sure I *will* open it—or live in it."

"Lena thinks you will."

"We'll see," she said with a smile.

"They're beginning the dancing," the young man said. "I've been waiting patiently."

"Then I mustn't refuse you." She let him lead her over to an area on the patio where a circle for dancing had been cleared. She noticed that Sylvia and Carl were already dancing, and she couldn't help but see how right they looked in each other's arms. She had thought earlier that Carl would ask her for the first dance, since the occasion was in her honor. But instead he had chosen Sylvia for his partner. Trudy felt ashamed for the tiny feeling of jealousy that crept through her at the sight of them so close together. She knew she was being possessive without any right to be, and she tried to dismiss the whole thing from her mind.

But Tom wasn't going to allow her to do that. As they danced, he said, "That certain doctor seems to have found his ideal dancing partner."

"Yes," she said, trying to sound casual. "They do dance well together."

"Something rather special about them, as if they're really in tune."

Trudy liked Tom but resented this line of talk. "She'll be returning to New York and her husband soon, so then she'll have to dance to a different tune."

"Interesting" was Tom's comment.

Trudy made an attempt to enliven things by saying, "Here I've been expecting you to say what a wonderful experience it is to have me in your arms, and all you do is talk about Carl and Sylvia!"

He gave a small moan, held her closer and admitted, "What a clod I am! Sorry!"

"Forgiven. As long as there are no relapses."

"Being here with you is sheer heaven," he murmured in her ear. "I can't believe my luck."

"You dance very well," she told him. "In fact, you seem to do a lot of things very well."

"I do a lot of small things pretty well, but I lose out on the really important matters."

"I can't believe that," she said as they continued to dance.

"Look around you. What do you see? Millionaires and their ladies. And I'm an interloper, just a poor newspaper writer."

She smiled up at him. "Oh, that's it! You want to be rich!"

"I *need* to be rich," he said. "I have expensive tastes."

"Maybe your book on Lena will make you wealthy."

"Like the kind of money Steiburn has? You're joking. No, I'll never be one of this crowd."

She gave him a teasing look. "Perhaps you could marry one of them."

"I've thought of that, but it wouldn't work. I have just enough integrity not to marry someone I'm not in love with. I make a rotten fortune hunter."

"But a lovely dancer," she said, laughing, as the music came to an end.

He escorted her off the patio. "Sorry I went into that line of gloomy speculation."

"I didn't mind. I feel a little like you said. I haven't received my inheritance yet."

Tom smiled. "But you will, and that's the difference. Though I doubt that it means anything much to you."

"I'm still pretty confused," she admitted.

The young writer glanced over his shoulder uneasily. "Lena's alone. I'd better get back to her, or she'll throw me off the book. We'll dance again later."

"Yes," she said, watching him go over to the actress and thinking that she liked him a lot.

Benson Steiburn came up to her with a giant of a man in tow and said, "Someone you've been waiting to meet, my dear! Giuseppe Pascal, this is Miss Trudy Stone."

The big man, neatly dressed in a white dinner jacket and black tie, moved forward and took her hand. A smile beamed on his swarthy moon-shaped face. She saw that he had rather good, even features under a head of unruly black curly hair, and she was sure he weighed at least two hundred and fifty pounds.

"Forgive my being so late," he said in perfect English.

She smiled. "You are a few days behind schedule."

He raised a pudgy hand. "You have no idea! The social season in Genoa is just beginning, and I'm on so many committees."

"Well, at least you are here now."

"I will see you at my office in Lerici tomorrow," he told her. "Will two in the afternoon suit you?"

"I'm sure I can be there then," she said. "I'm anxious to get the keys to the villa. I've heard many conflicting reports about it."

"You shall have the keys tomorrow," he promised.

"I've also had some strange and unpleasant experiences since I arrived here."

His heavy black eyebrows raised. "Don't tell me that Benson Steiburn is not a satisfactory host?"

"The best," she assured him. "But in spite of that, some odd things have happened."

"You must tell me all about them tomorrow," Pascal said. "Just now I thirst and know the pangs of hunger."

"Please don't let me detain you."

"Julia was my most beloved client," he told her. "I shall devote myself to you." Then he bowed and made his way toward the food table.

At that point Carl came across to her, a smile on his face. "Well, how do you like Pascal?"

"I find him overwhelming," she said, laughing.

"He is rather large," the doctor agreed. "I hope he still has a few wits about him and that he'll look after your affairs properly."

"I hope so, too. He wants to see me at his office in Lerici tomorrow at two."

"I'll drive you there," Carl offered.

"You're sure Mr. Steiburn won't mind?"

"He'll want me to do it." Then, as a pleasant waltz began, he asked her if she would like to dance.

She smiled her acceptance and they moved to the patio. Soon the small dance area was filled with others waltzing. She was both conscious that Carl was an excellent dancer and amazed at how happy she suddenly felt.

He said softly in her ear, "The waltz is a dance of love. It's right that it should be our dance. I've been thinking a lot about you today."

"I expected you to be too busy today for any kind of thoughts."

"I mean it," he said. "I think I've fallen a little bit in love with you. What more can I say?"

"Nothing more is needed," she replied with gentle amusement. "I'll file your message and give it my attention as soon as possible."

"Don't let it be too long," he said.

The waltz went on, and she enjoyed it thoroughly. When it was over, he said, "That's only the first installment. I'll expect other dances later."

He left her and rejoined Sylvia, who was with a group that included the stout Italian dignitary and his wife. Then Adrian Romitelli came up to Trudy and bowed.

"We haven't danced yet," he said.

"The evening has only begun."

Adrian looked annoyed as he told her, "Maybe, but you've somehow managed to dance with the men you admire most, Redman and that fellow Clarendon."

She felt her cheeks burn and looked around, hoping to find someone who would rescue her. But no one seemed to notice her plight.

She told Adrian, "We'll have a dance soon, I promise you."

"I don't like to see you hurt."

These words seemed strange, coming from him. "Oh?" she said.

"You have a very good chance of that happening," he said with some smugness.

"Thank you for your concern. But I believe I can take care of myself."

"You only think you can. By the way, where are Sylvia and Carl?"

"Somewhere around," she said. "Why?"

"I don't see them. Shall we take a little stroll? Move away from the lights and all this noise?"

Ordinarily she would have refused him, but she did have a slight headache, and the prospect of a walk sounded good. "Perhaps," she said. "Where will we go?"

"Over by the villa, your place." Adrian took her by the arm, and they slowly made their way through the crowded garden. Once they had reached the cool darkness, Trudy felt better.

"This is a lovely change. I'm glad you thought of it."

Adrian's thin face showed a satisfied smile. "I'm not totally a loss."

"Of course you're not," she said, wishing it were Carl with her instead of Adrian. Carl, who only a short while ago had whispered that he loved her.

"Your villa looks dark and lonely," Adrian remarked as they came near it.

"I plan to go through it tomorrow or the next day. Perhaps I will bring it to life again."

"Perhaps. If the masked swordsman approves of you."

"I don't believe that legend," she said defiantly.

"You might be wise to. This folklore is built on strong foundations." Then he halted as they were about to turn the corner of the villa, which would bring them to the swimming pool. He took a step ahead, glancing around the building at the pool. Then he came back to her.

Puzzled by his behavior, she asked, "What is it?"

"I expected something like this," he said quietly. He led her forward so that she could see Sylvia and Carl in each other's arms, standing at the distant end of the pool.

CHAPTER SEVEN

TRUDY'S EYES MOISTENED with tears as she stared at the couple, so engaged in each other that they were unaware of anyone's watching them. After a few seconds she turned and went around the corner of the villa, leaving the revealing scene behind her. Adrian was at her side.

"I'm sorry you had to witness that," he said in his suave way. "But it is time you knew the truth about Dr. Redman."

Badly hurt as she was and certain that Carl had cruelly led her on and lied to her, she was not about to let Adrian know that. Or give him the pleasure of gloating over her.

They were halfway back to the party before she halted and looked at him soberly. "You have the wrong impression about Dr. Redman and me. We're merely friends. If he is continuing a romance with Sylvia, it is no business of mine."

Her companion's face showed surprise. "But I thought—" He left the sentence unfinished.

"I have no idea what you thought," she said, working hard to keep her tone free of emotion. "I suggest we both forget about it—forget we saw anything."

"If that is what you wish."

"It is. While I'm a guest of Mr. Steiburn's, I have no desire to cause trouble for him or his daughter."

"Very well," he said. Then he added self-righteously, "I only wanted you to know for your own sake."

"I won't forget that," she said in a manner that concealed her true feelings. Achieving a voice devoid of expression was not easy when she was torn by the revelation that Carl was a shallow person and that Sylvia was not truly a friend.

As they rejoined the party in the rose gardens, the music was still playing, and many people were dancing on the patio. Among them Trudy saw Lena Morel with Tom Clarendon. Tom was being his usual charming self, and Lena was actually smiling, which made her look younger and more like the radiant film star she had once been.

Romitelli could not resist saying sourly, "I see your other admirer is busy dancing with his owner."

Trudy gave him a bitter smile. "You have a wicked tongue, Adrian."

"I don't embroider the truth," he replied.

"No. You offer it with a knife in the back. Didn't you say you wished to dance with me?"

"Yes," he said, somewhat flustered at her sudden suggestion. "Anything to improve your poor picture of me."

"I'm afraid that picture is engraved in my mind," she said with an arch smile as they moved onto the patio.

She felt little like dancing, and though Adrian danced well enough, she spent the time waiting for the music to end. She said nothing as they made their way around the dance circle. When they passed Lena and Tom, everyone exchanged the usual polite greetings, and Trudy thought it had turned out to be a very strange evening.

The music ended, but Adrian did not leave her side. She found it hard to talk with him and looked about for some means of escape. It soon came in the massive form of Giuseppe Pascal.

"May I have a few words with you in private?" he asked.

Adrian bowed stiffly and said, "Thank you for the dance, Miss Stone." Then he moved on to the bar.

Trudy gave the lawyer a grateful smile. "Thank you for coming to my rescue," she said.

"I would have done it sooner had I noticed. Romitelli is a bit of a scoundrel and a bore."

"He is not the sort you seek out."

The big man chuckled. "Yet your aunt did just that. He was almost constantly in her company."

Trudy was surprised and fascinated to hear this. "He told me that, but I couldn't believe it."

"It is true," Pascal said. "I knew he had borrowed a great deal of money from her, which he had no intention of paying back. I warned her about him. But her reply was that she felt sorry for him, and he was a luxury she could afford."

"Incredible!"

"Not really. Women alone, as your aunt was in her last years, are sometimes desperate for companionship. Romitelli offered her that."

Trudy nodded. "In that case, there isn't much one can say."

"I made no attempt to break them up," the lawyer said. "Julia knew what she was doing and the sort of man he was. I think it has been hard for him since her death."

"Because he's been shut off from that source of money?" Trudy ventured.

"Exactly," he agreed.

"He does give the impression of being rather desperate. He doesn't appear to have any regular income."

"He gambles and occasionally makes some money that way. I wouldn't care to be in a game with him," Pascal said knowingly.

"I'm surprised my aunt didn't leave him some money."

The big man shrugged. "I was also surprised when I read her will. And I have no doubt he thinks he was cheated."

"You believe that?"

"The fellow considers himself handsome and a prize for any lady. He probably feels he gave a lot of his time to Julia and she neglected to reward him."

"Perhaps because she gave him money so freely when she was alive."

"Perhaps. Or there could be another reason. I'll discuss that tomorrow when we have our meeting."

"I'm looking forward to it," she said.

The music began again, and the lawyer insisted she dance with him. In spite of his size, he was astonishingly light on his feet. For a few minutes Trudy forgot the cares of the evening and truly enjoyed herself.

When the music stopped, she found Carl standing there, waiting for her. He nodded to Pascal, who moved away, and said, "I've been looking for you."

"Have you?" she asked. "Where?"

"Everywhere. The last I saw of you was when you were talking to Romitelli."

"You seemed to be missing from the party for a while," she said, watching him closely.

His face crimsoned. "Yes, I know. Sylvia had a bad headache. She worked too hard today to make this party for you a success. I took a little walk with her."

"So considerate of you," Trudy said with scarcely veiled irony. "But then you have always been close to Sylvia."

Carl continued to look embarrassed. "Sylvia is like a younger sister to me."

"Weren't you once engaged? I think you told me about it." She asked the question casually.

He shifted position awkwardly. "That was a long time ago—before we really understood what we wanted. We're merely good friends now."

"I'm sure you are," she said, with a small smile.

The music had started up again, and he asked, "May I have this dance?"

"I'm afraid I've promised it to someone else," she said. It wasn't true, but he didn't have to know that.

"I'm sorry. A little later, then?"

"Of course."

Luckily, Tom Clarendon came over to her at that moment with a warm smile on his face. Without a word, he took her in his arms and they began to dance. His timely arrival made him doubly welcome.

"I was sure Redman was going to claim you as a partner before I reached you," Tom said.

She smiled. "He asked me, but I refused."

"Good for you!" Tom sounded pleased. "Because he's a doctor and has charm, nearly all the females around here fall all over themselves to please him."

"I try to avoid doing anything like that."

"A female of spirit. Lena likes you, and that's why, I'm sure."

"She doesn't mind your dancing with me?"

"She told me to. Lena is a realist. She knows she's too old for me. By this time in the evening, she prefers to relax and watch the dancing."

"She's looking exceptionally well tonight," Trudy said.

"Tell her," he urged. "It could mean a lot to her."

So when the dance ended, she walked back to where Lena was seated. The older woman gave her a swift appraisal and said, "That dress exactly suits you."

Tom laughed. "Trudy has come over to congratulate you, and as usual, you got in first."

"That doesn't matter," Trudy said. "I think you look wonderful tonight, Miss Morel. And your dress is also lovely."

"Thank you, dear," Lena said. "At my age, compliments are rare and I value them. And please call me Lena." She glanced at Tom. "Trudy reminds me so much of poor Julia. What a pity Julia didn't bring her over here when she was alive."

The writer agreed.

The former film star gave Trudy a wise look. "I often wonder if I wasn't Julia's only true friend. So many of the others used her, like that Romitelli."

"At least he made no pretense about it," Trudy said.

"Be careful of him," Tom warned. "He'll be trying to latch onto you once you have your money."

"Another word of caution," Lena Morel said. "Despite this party and everything else, remember that Benson Steiburn is eager to get his hands on the villa."

"I know," Trudy said. That fact had been looming larger in her mind ever since she'd come upon Carl and Sylvia in each other's arms. It seemed likely that Sylvia, her father and Carl could all be playing a game to oust her from the villa. Perhaps that was the explanation for the weird happenings and the appearance of the masked swordsman.

She glanced across the garden and, by sheer coincidence, saw the three of them talking together. This only served to reinforce what she'd been thinking.

The evening wore on, and she danced with many of the male guests, some of whom spoke little or no English. At midnight the party ended. After the guests had been seen on their way, Sylvia came up to her in the garden, deserted now except for the servants clearing up. With a smile on her face, she asked, "Did you have a good time?"

Trudy managed to smile in return. "Yes. It was a most interesting evening."

"I wanted it to be. You've had too many problems since you've arrived here."

"Let us hope there are no more." She paused, then asked, "Will you be returning to New York and your husband soon?"

For just a moment, there was a wary look on Sylvia's face. Then she quickly recovered and said, "I may not be able to get away as soon as I'd like. Father wants me to attend an art auction in Rome next month."

"I thought Carl did all the art buying for him," Trudy said.

Sylvia offered her another smile. "When I'm here I often accompany him as a sort of adviser."

"I see," she said. "I didn't know."

"This is an important auction," Sylvia told her. "Some fine Italian painters will be represented there."

"What will your husband say?"

Sylvia shrugged. "He won't mind. After all, he does work for my father. So he understands."

"I'm sure he does."

After thanking her again, Trudy went up to her room. She felt weary very suddenly; the excitement of the night had kept her stimulated, but now the full impact of the evening hit her. And her disillusionment with Carl Redman was part of her fatigue.

As she prepared for bed, she speculated on Sylvia's change of plans about leaving. It almost suggested that Carl had asked her to remain. He might have been persuading her when he'd held her in his arms by the pool. Even Sylvia's father had indicated some uneasiness about her marriage. Had it become only a sham? And were Sylvia and Carl lovers again?

Trudy shut off the lamp and slid into bed. She saw herself as young and naive, unable to cope with these wealthy and sophisticated people. But she must learn—and quickly. It was only a matter of hours before she'd hear the contents of her aunt's will and inherit a large fortune of her own, along with the villa.

How easy it could have been for Carl, Sylvia or even Steiburn himself to try to frighten her with those weird tricks. She determined that she would not give in to them.

She fell asleep with her mind troubled by these unpleasant thoughts. The inevitable result was a series of nightmares. In one of them she was alone in the gardens, and the masked swordsman stepped out of the bushes and blocked her way. When she attempted to escape him, he grasped her by the arms and held her captive. She screamed at him and waited for the moment when she was able to get one hand free. Then she clawed at the wide black mask and pulled it down—to reveal the face of Carl Redman!

At that point she woke up with a small cry. She stared into the darkness and, in her fright, groped for the switch on the bedside table lamp. She was rewarded with a small glow of light that reduced her terror. Seldom had a dream been more real to her. Had it been a message? Was it Carl who'd been playing the role of the masked swordsman? It had seemed all too real in her nightmare.

After a long while she slipped off into a light sleep, but again she was plagued by dreams. This time she saw the pale death mask of her aunt Julia floating through the air, then coming directly toward her in a terrifying way.

She wakened again. By now dawn was beginning to show. She had one more brief nap and then got up and dressed for breakfast.

She had breakfast alone. The maid told her the others had eaten earlier. She was having her second cup of coffee when Benson Steiburn came into the breakfast room.

"Good morning," he said. "I was hoping I might find you here."

"I slept later than I planned to," she apologized.

"No matter," he said with a wave of his hand. He looked every inch the country gentleman today in a brown-checked suit. "I hope you had a good time."

"It was a wonderful party."

He stood by the large window staring out at the side lawn and the villa. He rubbed his beard, as he often did when he was under tension, then he turned to her with a slight frown on his face. "A rather strange thing happened last night," he said with more than a little awkwardness.

She was watching him closely. "Really?" she asked.

He nodded. "Actually it has to do with the villa."

"With the villa?" she echoed, wondering if this was to be some new tale to try to turn her against her legacy.

"Well, not really about the villa," he amended. "I should say it's about the pool over at the villa."

It was her turn to become tense. Was he going to tell her about the love scene between Sylvia and Carl? Could he be so disturbed by their relationship that he was willing to confide in her?

"Aunt Julia's swimming pool?" she managed to say.

"Yes." His light blue eyes fixed on her. "And about your aunt, as well."

"What do you mean?" she asked anxiously.

He hesitated. "Well, one of the servants went by the pool this morning. He found something floating in it and brought it to me."

"What was it?"

The older man looked perplexed and fingered his beard once again. "I must warn you, this is very strange."

"Please go on," she insisted, still uncertain if he was going to divulge what had taken place between Sylvia and Carl.

"The man found a fancy party shawl floating on the surface of Julia's pool. It struck him that someone at the party might have strolled over there and lost it without realizing its loss."

"A party shawl in the pool?" Trudy began to tremble.

"Yes," he said. "I was sure it looked familiar, so I showed it to Sylvia. She recognized it at once as a shawl that Julia often wore."

Trudy stared at him. "How would it get into the pool?"

"I have no idea. I'm merely passing on the information to you."

"It's weird!" she exclaimed. "That pool seems to be a haven for mystery."

"It could be that one of the guests had a similar shawl," Steiburn said. "But I don't recall seeing it last night."

"Perhaps someone stole it from the villa when those paintings were taken," Trudy suggested.

"Entirely possible. But why throw it in the pool?"

Trudy couldn't keep the sarcasm out of her voice. "Well, perhaps it's another ghostly event. Maybe my dead aunt was out there watching the party, and when someone came close, she ran off, discarding her shawl in the pool. Just another macabre reason for my having nothing to do with the villa.''

Steiburn shook his head. "I don't blame you for being annoyed. I wasn't going to tell you, but then I felt I should.''

"Thank you," she said dryly. "It would appear Aunt Julia's ghost has come to join that of the masked swordsman.''

"I'm sure there is some rational explanation for it, and I promise you we'll find it.''

"What does Sylvia think about it?''

"My daughter is just as bewildered as we are.''

"And Carl?''

"He hasn't seen it yet. He left very early this morning on estate business. I understand he is driving you to Lerici this afternoon.''

Trudy rose from the table. "I don't want to put him to all that trouble. I'm almost certain I can make some other arrangement.''

"I will not hear of it," Steiburn protested. "I insist you let him take you.''

Trudy would have preferred not to have to be in the company of the doctor, but she found it awkward to refuse the older man's generosity. So she agreed to let Carl drive her to Pascal's office.

She went up to her room and was surprised to find Sylvia there, seated in a chair, waiting for her. She said, "It's funny, but I was going to see if I could find you.''

Sylvia gave her a bright smile. "Our thoughts were in tune.''

"So it seems. I heard about the shawl. Where is it?"

"I gave it to the man downstairs who takes our things to the dry cleaners. It was soiled and already may be ruined by being in the pool."

"You recognized it as Julia's?"

"Absolutely. It's a lovely shawl, pale blue with a lot of colorful embroidery. I even mentioned it to her once."

"How do you suppose it got into the pool?" Trudy asked, keeping a sharp eye on the other woman.

"I don't know." Sylvia sighed. "Unless Julia gave it to Lena Morel. She sometimes did give her clothes. Lena might have had it with her last night, and somehow it fell into the pool."

"I didn't see her with it. And I particularly noted what she was wearing."

"Then its presence will remain a mystery, I fear."

"Like so many other things here" was Trudy's quiet comment.

"Don't let the incident spoil last night for you," Sylvia urged. "One of the servants could have stolen it. There are all sorts of possibilities."

"I realize that," Trudy acknowledged.

"Carl was disappointed that you danced so little with him at the party," Sylvia remarked.

"I'm sorry about that, but I had to spread myself around. You had so many guests."

Sylvia nodded. "I'm sure Carl is fond of you. I mean, really fond."

It seemed to Trudy that Sylvia was deliberately trying to cover up her own relationship with Carl. What better way than to pretend she believed he was especially interested in Trudy? And he had surely played his part to make Trudy believe the same thing.

"We'll gradually get to know each other better," Trudy said carefully, hoping she sounded noncommittal.

"He thinks he knows you pretty well now. You'll have a chance to spend more time with him on the drive to Lerici today."

Trudy nodded but made no comment to this.

"Well, I must be on my way," the dark-haired young woman said with a smile as she stood up. "I hope all goes well with the reading of the will."

TRUDY HAD A LIGHT SNACK at twelve-thirty, then went upstairs to change into a gray silk dress and gray shoes. At about one-fifteen she went out. Carl was waiting for her by the white convertible.

In a casual beige jacket and pants, and a dark blue cotton turtleneck, he looked even more dashing than usual. He opened the car door for her with a smile. "You look great!" he said. "You'll turn Pascal's head."

She laughed. "Today I want him to concentrate on his work, not on me."

Carl slid behind the wheel. "You're much too attractive, do you know that?"

"Men say that to every girl they meet."

"Not this man," he told her as they drove off.

"You're not starved for beauty here," she said. "What about Sylvia? She is truly lovely."

Carl gave her a quick glance. "Why bring her into it?"

"I'm merely pointing out there are lots of attractive females around. And what is more, I'm certain you are aware of it."

He frowned slightly as he guided the sleek white car onto the main highway. "You seem to be trying to make me out a womanizer."

"Aren't you?"

"I don't think so," he told her, giving her a short, sober glance. "I admire women and I care for women. My general interest ends there. I am a medical doctor."

"Who works at his profession only very little."

"I still know who I am," he said. "And I hope that will always be true."

Trudy knew she was giving him a fairly hard time, but she felt only a small guilt about it. What he had done the previous night had been infinitely more cruel.

She sat back and admired the beautiful view of the ocean as they drove along the broad highway. After a short silence, broken only by the humming of the motor, she said, "I wonder how I'll make out at the reading of the will."

"You know everything that's in it already," Carl said.

"Not actually. I've just been told I'm Aunt Julia's chief heir. I don't know who else may have been named. But I do know Adrian wasn't. Pascal told me that much. And I hear he's very upset."

"He spends most of his time feeling upset," Carl said disgustedly.

They reached the outskirts of Lerici, which Trudy found to be much like Palina, except that it had more pastel-colored cottages. The palm trees thrived along the streets, and the business section was slightly larger than that of Palina. Carl finally brought the car to a halt before a beige stucco building with signs for a number of professional offices.

Carl opened the car door for her and asked, "Do you want me to come up with you?"

She hesitated. "No, I think I'd better do this alone."

"Okay. Pascal is on the second floor, in an office at the rear of the building."

"Thanks," she said with a small smile. "I'll find it."

"I'll do a few errands and come back and wait for you right here."

She nodded. "Thanks again." As she made her way briskly across the sidewalk and into the building, she heard him drive off. A tinge of regret went through her as she thought of how, under different circumstances, she would have wanted him to be with her at this critical time.

CHAPTER EIGHT

THE UPPER HALLWAY was narrow and rather dark, with an odor of dampness pervading everything. Trudy walked past several closed doors and continued on to the end of the hall. The drab atmosphere brought back the sinister forebodings that had haunted her earlier.

She saw the lawyer's name on the door ahead and approached it tensely. She knocked, and the voice of Giuseppe Pascal invited her to come in. She found herself in a tiny office. The huge lawyer was seated behind a small desk in the middle of the room.

His swarthy face showed a smile as he rose slowly to greet her. "You found me," he said. "Very good." He pulled a chair out from the wall and placed it before his desk for her to sit in.

She noted that the single window of the office looked out at the windows of another shabby building. The tiny room wasn't lavishly furnished in any way, though there was a strong aroma of food present. She suspected he might have been eating when she knocked and had quickly stuffed his lunch in some convenient drawer of the desk.

"Sit down, please, Miss Stone," he said in his excellent English.

Trudy sat opposite him and said, "Dr. Redman told me what floor you were on."

"Ah, yes, he is familiar with my office." The stout man was wearing a rather soiled white suit, and his bulging stomach rested on the edge of the desk. "It was a most enjoyable party last night. Steiburn makes an excellent host."

"I agree," she said.

Pascal studied her with obvious interest. Then he said, "So now we come to the business for which you have traveled so far."

"I am a long way from home," she said.

The big man smiled. "But now Palina and the villa are your home."

"I'm sure it will take a while to find myself actually feeling that way."

"Of course." He nodded. "I will spare you the entire will, a long and tedious document. It is available to you for scrutiny at any time. I propose to give you just the main elements."

"I'm most curious to know what the will stipulates," she said.

"Well, have no fears, you are named the sole heir. Which means that at a modest estimate, you are now worth several million American dollars."

"That much!" Trudy exclaimed, going pale. "I had no idea Aunt Julia was so wealthy!"

"Not all of it is readily liquid, however. Much of it is invested in long-term bonds and in various businesses. But your annual income will be sizeable."

"No one else was left anything?" she asked, puzzled.

"That is correct," the lawyer said. "She wanted you to have it all. At least, during your lifetime."

Something in his tone when he said those words alerted her. She repeated carefully, "In my lifetime?"

He nodded. "As long as you live."

"May I ask what happens to the money after my death? I assumed when the estate was bequeathed to me it was a gift for all time."

Giuseppe Pascal beamed at her as he explained, "A gift to you for your lifetime."

"And after that?"

"It goes to someone else."

Trudy was stunned. "Someone else? Who, may I ask?"

"You may ask, but I cannot tell you," he said.

Trudy was becoming increasingly upset. "I have every right to know!"

"I agree, but I cannot offer you the information because I do not know myself."

"You can't be serious!"

"I wish I weren't." The fat man sighed. "The will was drawn up by my father before his death. There is a second will in a sealed envelope that states the name of the heir following you and the terms of the settlement on him or her."

"A second will?" she gasped.

"I was as shocked as you when your aunt explained the details of her bequest. But it makes no difference. You are alive and will continue to be the heir up to the moment of your death."

Trudy was trying to get the true meaning of this straight in her mind. "You're telling me I'm to be a temporary heiress? That when I die, the estate will go to someone else—someone not of my choosing?"

"You have phrased it very well," Pascal said with admiration.

"This has to be some sort of macabre joke! Aunt Julia could not have been serious!"

"I assure you, she was," he said. "And so that is how it stands."

"This is very different from what I expected," she told him. "So I'm an interim heir."

"You could call yourself that. Still, you will have the full benefit of your aunt's fortune while you are alive."

"Can I do what I like with the money? Am I authorized to sell the villa if I wish?"

"You are free to handle the cash assets as you like," Pascal said. "The villa is another matter."

"Oh?"

He nodded in his ponderous fashion. "I regret to say the will stipulates that you must keep the villa and maintain it."

She protested, "That isn't fair. I'll have a New York lawyer fight the will."

He spread his huge hands in a gesture of resignation. "You may do that, but I question whether you will be successful under Italian law."

"What about my seeing the villa?" she asked.

"I have the keys right here." He opened a drawer and brought out a ring of several keys and passed them across to her.

"If I'm expected to live at the villa, I must have a staff," she said as she took the keys.

"I regret that the old staff is scattered. Some of them were not trustworthy in any case. They stole many art objects before I dismissed them and shut up the villa."

She sighed. "The will states I must keep the villa and maintain it but it does not say I have to live there?"

"That is right." Pascal smiled. "And if I were in your place, I would settle for a minimum maintenance and let it remain closed, while you may live wherever it pleases you."

She laughed without mirth. "Turn it over to the masked swordsman?"

"If you like," he said. "You have heard about the legendary ghost?"

"I have done better than that," she said grimly. "I have seen him." And she explained what had happened.

When she had finished, the lawyer said, "Most interesting!"

"Before I leave, I'd like to ask you one other thing. Your father drew up these wills, so you're not aware of the contents of the other one. But did my aunt give you any hint at all as to who might benefit by my death?"

The big man looked wary. "I tried to find that out," he said. "She was evasive. But she did drop a hint or two."

"Such as?"

"She once said Romitelli knew more than anyone else about her and her affairs. That could be interpreted as a way of saying he also knew about her second will."

Trudy nodded. "He was close to her."

"The other thing she said was that the person who would get her fortune after you was someone whom she cared for a great deal."

"And what did you gather from that?"

Pascal folded his hands on his oversized stomach and looked at her silently for a moment. Then he said, "It could be one of many people. But I think chiefly of Adrian Romitelli or perhaps Carl Redman."

With a tiny gasp, she said, "Why those two?"

"She had hinted Romitelli knew the contents of her second will, so I'm almost convinced he is the heir named in it. As we discussed last night, he was not mentioned in the first will in any way, though she knew he needed money."

The fat man's logic was convincing. "I'm sure you are right," she said.

"I'm glad you agree with me. Cash will be available in the Palina bank in your name. In the meanwhile, I would not rush into doing anything."

"I haven't much choice," she said ruefully. "I feel I am imposing on Mr. Steiburn."

"He enjoys having house guests," Pascal said. "And you know he covets the villa."

"Yes," she said, her lovely face shadowing. "The fact that I'm not authorized to sell it won't be good news for him."

"Let him work on it," the lawyer suggested. "He has an entire law firm in Rome at his disposal. If anyone can find a weak spot in the terms of the will, I'd say it would be Steiburn."

"I'll remember that," she said, rising.

"I'll be returning to Genoa tomorrow," he told her, struggling to his feet. "But I'm always available. Call on me when you feel you need me."

The interview ended on this note. Trudy left his office in a more confused state than when she'd arrived. It appeared that unless she could make a successful appeal, her legacy was a lot less than she had expected. The idea that Adrian might be the heir in the event of her death was a little terrifying, for she realized how desperate the man was for money and how unpleasant he could be.

Pascal had named Carl Redman as the other possible heir if she died. But whatever her suspicions were of the doctor's integrity, she did not think her aunt had named him as a beneficiary of the second will. For one thing, he was clearly in no need of funds, he had an excellent position with Steiburn. If he ever left the art collector, he could easily practice medicine elsewhere. Against this was Carl's admission that he loved the life-style he had now. And he seemed to be carrying on an affair with Sylvia while protesting it wasn't so.

When she stepped out into the Mediterranean sunshine again, she saw Carl leaning against the hood of the car, his eyes fixed on the office-building door. On seeing her, he smiled and went around and opened the car door for her.

As they drove away, he asked, "How did it go?"

"I hardly know what to say," she replied. Then she told him about the first will and the second one in the event of her death. She mentioned that Adrian was likely the person named as the second heir, without revealing that the lawyer had also included Carl's name as a possible beneficiary.

Carl scowled as they followed the highway along the shore. "It's monstrous! You must get a lawyer to contest it!"

"Pascal thinks my best bet would be to turn the problem over to Benson Steiburn. He feels Steiburn can wield more power than any lawyer I find in New York."

"A good suggestion," Carl agreed. "Pascal may be fat and fond of partying, but he is no fool."

"I'm certain of that. And Steiburn has an interest in it all, since he would like to buy the villa."

"Exactly." Carl glanced at her. "You look done in. I'm going to park ahead by the beach for a little while. The air and the sunshine will do you good."

She was too upset to protest. Actually, the idea didn't sound all that displeasing. She was in no need to hurry back, and he didn't seem to be worried about the time.

They parked facing the beach and the ocean. Quite a few people were scattered along the soft white sand, and the sun on the ocean gave it a flashing emerald hue.

Trudy let out a relaxed sigh and sat back against the leather seat, then gazed up at the almost cloudless sky. "Nothing can spoil this moment," she said with feeling.

The wind rustled slightly through Carl's hair as he said, "It is perhaps one of the loveliest corners of the world."

"I'm beginning to believe that," she said. "I almost think I was starting to plan to open the villa and live there."

"You can still do it."

She smiled wryly. "I'd feel like a tenant, not an owner. No, as things stand now, it has been spoiled for me."

"Don't make any rash decisions," the doctor advised.

She smiled at him. "Another bit of advice Pascal gave me."

"Good," he said. "I'd like to be with you when you visit the villa for the first time."

"I'll go there after lunch."

"May I accompany you?"

"Can you spare the time?"

"Easily."

"All right. After lunch, then." She knew that with him being with her, she'd feel much more happy about the whole business. An inner voice told her to go slow, not to put a lot of trust in this very likable man who had turned out to be a deceiver. But her need for someone more than balanced her fears.

He studied her, his gray eyes sober. "You know, in spite of everything, I believe this will turn out well for you."

"I wonder," she said, staring out at the ocean. "I suppose Tom and Lena Morel swim from a beach like this."

"Yes, they do. They go every day the weather permits. She dislikes pools and loves to swim."

"Tom invited me to join them. I must go one day."

"You like Tom, don't you?" Carl asked.

Trudy glanced at him with amusement. "Of course I like him, but that doesn't mean I'm madly in love with him."

He was serious. "I think you have more than a casual interest in him."

"I haven't thought that much about it."

"Lena has a great hold on him," Carl said. "He needs to do that book on her."

"It will help her even more than it will benefit him," she argued.

"Possibly. I noticed he gave you a lot of attention at the party last night."

"Did you?" she said. And then, remembering the tender love scene she caught him in with Sylvia, she couldn't resist teasing him by adding, "I remember you told me last night you loved me a little."

He nodded, then said quietly, "I probably did. You know how I feel about you."

"Not truly," she said, rushing on now that she had the advantage. "Let's say I know what you *tell* me you feel, but that may not be what you truly *do* feel."

"Now you're beginning to talk as you did earlier— a lot of silly mumbo jumbo," he protested. "As if you were angry with me."

"Sorry," she said with a smile.

"I don't believe you are," he replied, returning her smile. "But I'll take you at your word, more than you do for me. And I'm also going to take you to lunch here in Lerici, at a very special place."

"Sounds lovely. Where?"

"You know that Shelley loved this area?"

"Yes, you told me that my first day here. Shelley drowned nearby, and when his body washed ashore, his wife burned it on the beach in a funeral pyre."

Carl nodded, looking pleased. "You have it correct. We are going to the Hotel Shelley e della Palmo. They have excellent food, and the dining area looks out over the water."

Within a quarter hour they had reached the modest-sized hotel. Carl was known there, and the headwaiter showed them to a prime table in the garden restaurant, situated on an upper outdoor patio and offering an excellent view of the ocean. Carl assured her that the best of the many fine dishes offered was scampi with mustard sauce and crepes suzette.

As they sipped wine prior to their entrées being served, she told him, "I love this place! I must come here again."

He smiled at her. "Not you and Tom. I couldn't stand that. At night with candlelight it's terribly romantic—and dangerous."

"Have you been here with Sylvia?"

He looked startled and then managed a laugh. "Of course. I told you, it's a special place."

"You have shared so many things, and yet you went your own way in the end."

"That happens more often than you think." And then, in what she felt might have been a deliberate effort to change the subject, he told her, "What worries me is the likelihood of Romitelli's being the one named in the other will."

"Go on," she said.

"You know he's strange and hard up for money."

"Yes."

Carl's expression was grave. "Some people in his position do awful things to get their hands on cash. I believe he's capable of being a threat to you."

She smiled wanly. "Are you suggesting he might wish my death a trifle sooner than nature intended, so he can benefit from the will?"

"I'm suggesting that if he gets desperate enough, he might try to have you killed."

"We don't even know he is named in the will!" she protested.

"If Pascal thinks so, I'd accept it."

"Please," she begged him, "don't spoil this lovely lunch with that sort of talk. Time enough to worry about it later."

"All right," he said soberly. "But you mustn't forget it."

The luncheon was as nearly perfect as anything could be. A good two hours had passed before they were on the road again. Satiated with good food and wine, Trudy lay back dreamily against the seat as Carl drove. She decided he was a charming deceiver, which was just a little better than being an ordinary one. She felt that he was fond of her, despite his love affair with Sylvia. And she wondered if and when the pretty, dark girl would leave her father's house and return to America and her husband.

When they reached the castle, they found that both Benson Steiburn and his daughter had gone golfing. They decided to take a little time to freshen up and then meet at the entrance to the villa.

Trudy changed into her jeans and a dark shirt. She had no idea what condition the villa might be in, so she didn't want to wear anything that might be soiled easily. She made sure she had the keys and the flashlight she'd used before, and found another, rather battered flashlight for Carl, in case he didn't think of bringing one. Then she went down to join him.

He was nowhere around, so she strolled over to the villa on her own. As she passed the swimming pool, she paused for a moment to stare into it. It was discolored and filled with leaves since it had fallen into disuse. She studied her reflection in the murky surface and again knew the strange feeling of fear and depression that she'd experienced previously.

Then she heard Carl call her, and she broke out of her reverie. As he came up to her, she held out the flashlights and keys. "You see I'm properly prepared," she said.

"Good," he said, taking the keys and the battered flashlight. "To the best of my knowledge, the electric system—which operates from the same plant as the one for the castle—is not in use."

"You may lead the way," she told him. "You've been in the villa before."

"Quite a few times," he admitted.

They used the main door, which took a fairly large key. As soon as Carl had opened the door inward and they'd entered the shadowed hallway, Trudy was greeted with the familiar musty smell of old houses that have been closed for a long time. She waited for her eyes to adjust to the gloom around her, then followed Carl into a huge room that might be considered a combination reception and living room.

Carl swung the beam of his flashlight about so she could see the walls and the columns supporting the balcony that ran around the room at the second level.

"There are some fine paintings still hanging here, and a great deal of the original furniture is here, too." He put his hand on the edge of a large table with a white marble top.

"It must have been magnificent," she said. "And you say it so badly needs repairs it ought to be demolished."

Carl nodded. "That is what Benson Steiburn's experts have told him."

Trudy was thinking it might be worthwhile to protect the old villa. "Do you think he was told that because they knew it was what he wanted to hear?"

"To be fair, I hesitate to say," Carl admitted.

"It is more impressive than I expected."

"You've only had a glimpse at a portion of it. Let's take the grand stairway up to the next level."

She followed him up a curving marble staircase that led to the shallow balcony area overlooking the large room below. The balcony also gave access to the many rooms leading off it.

"Notice the Gothic windows," he said, pointing them out. "I'm afraid they are so dust-laden they let in little light at the moment."

"So many rooms up here!" she marveled.

"Your aunt only used one wing of the building," he said. "The room just ahead to the left was her bedroom."

Trudy found herself entering the large room with bated breath. She played her flashlight beam about and saw a wide bed with silk coverings and a giant oil painting on the wall above it. The dressers, chairs and chaise longue were antique, and shining despite their accumulated dust.

Carl said, "Perhaps she was right in wishing to save all this. Steiburn could find somewhere else for his museum."

"But he has his mind set on this place."

Just then there came a sound like the slamming of a door out on the balcony. They both turned and gazed in the direction from which the unexpected sound had come.

In a whisper, Carl said, "It seems we're not alone in here."

"Who could it be?" she whispered back.

"Maybe one of the servants who has been stealing things. You stay here a minute, and I'll go see what I can find out."

"Don't be too long," she urged.

He was already on his way out and a moment later had vanished into the darkness of the balcony. She stood there waiting and suddenly realized she was trembling. Not only that, but all those awful feelings of apprehension had returned, this time stronger than ever. She listened but could hear nothing.

The minutes went by, slowly, and she began to regret that she had agreed to let him venture out alone. They ought to have gone together. Separated as they were now, each of them was more vulnerable. She fought with herself to be patient, but it was a losing battle. She moved silently out the door onto the balcony.

It was all strangely still, a sinister quiet that sent a new chill of fear through her. She groped along, holding the flashlight high so she could see well ahead. Then all at once she stumbled over something. Even before she glanced down, she knew it was a body.

Trudy flashed the beam of light down and cried out in terror. It was Carl. He lay there motionless and white-faced. She knelt to examine him, and as she did, she heard a rustling sound behind her. With another sharp cry, she whirled around and saw, outlined by the beam of her flashlight, the figure of the masked swordsman.

She screamed and ran along the narrow corridor, the phantom behind her. She reached the marble steps and raced down, losing her balance about halfway to the bottom. The flashlight fell from her hand and clattered off as she struggled to maintain her balance and keep going. But the time she'd lost proved to be her undoing. Strong hands seized her and threw her down to the bottom of the stairs. The phantom figure came after her, and then she felt the pressure of powerful fingers closing over her throat.

CHAPTER NINE

"TRUDY!"

Vaguely she heard her name being called in an anguished tone and from a great distance. But her fight for breath under the strong fingers of her attacker was of much more immediate concern.

"Trudy!" The voice was closer now, but she was also near the point of losing consciousness.

Then, suddenly, the pressure was gone from her throat. She coughed and managed to take a few deep breaths; she wondered if she had died and if this were the first stage of death. Only at that instant did she realize the ghostly figure had left her.

"Trudy!" This time she recognized Carl's voice, a voice in torment. A moment later she saw him looming above her, his flashlight beam focusing on her head and shoulders.

"Carl!" she gasped hoarsely.

He knelt by her. "How badly hurt are you?"

She raised herself up on an elbow. "I'll be all right now."

"Do you feel well enough to get to your feet?" he asked.

She nodded and he helped her up. Then she told him what had happened. "When whoever it was heard you, he ran off."

"A moment earlier, and I'd have had him," Carl said grimly. "I was knocked out by a blow from someone who stalked me from behind. Obviously that was to set the stage for the attack on you."

"The person didn't count on your coming to as soon as you did, thank heaven."

Carl played the light from the flash all around the big room. "It's hard to be sure, but I doubt whoever it was is here now."

She gazed into the gloomy shadows of the spacious area and shuddered. "I want to leave!" she cried.

"I think that would be an excellent idea," he said, taking her arm and escorting her to the front door. When they left, he locked the padlock, though it seemed a futile gesture. Clearly, others had some means of entry to the villa.

Back at the castle, she carefully washed the spot at the back of Carl's head where he'd been hit, then put some ointment and tape over it.

He eyed her worriedly. "Your throat will be black-and-blue shortly. He very nearly strangled you. Did you get a good look at him?"

"Yes."

"Tell me everything you can remember."

"What can I tell you?" she asked in frustration. "It was the masked swordsman, wearing the black cloak and gloves."

"You have no idea who might have been concealed by the mask and cloak?"

"None at all," she said unhappily. "He looked just the same as he did before, when you said I hadn't seen him and I knew I had."

"Just let's worry about this incident," he told her. "I know the attack was real today, because I was one of the victims. And I'm certain we're dealing with someone who stole some of the valuable art from the villa."

She glanced down at her shirt and jeans, which were grimy from her fall. Her arms and legs ached, and there were some bruises evident. "It wasn't a warm welcoming party."

"You should go upstairs, take a hot bath and rest a little before the others return."

She agreed. Then she looked into his handsome, concerned face and said, "Thank you for saving my life."

"I need no thanks for that."

"I'm sure I would have died if you hadn't come along in time."

His smile was melancholy as he took her in his arms. "I was merely being selfish. Saving you for myself." He bent close and kissed her gently.

As she parted from him, she said, "We'll have a lot to tell Sylvia and her father."

"We surely will," he agreed.

She went up to her bedroom, took a bath and then went to bed. When her travel alarm sounded an hour later, she was still awake but felt rested. She quickly got up and dressed.

As she sat before the mirror completing her make-up, she thought about all that had happened. It seemed that whoever was playing the role of the masked swordsman was someone other than Carl. At least that much had been established. Carl, like her, had been attacked by a living person.

And Carl had surely rescued her from almost certain death. His attitude after the incident and his tender embrace made it plain he was carrying on the charade of loving her and wanting to be with her. But she knew that Sylvia was there between them.

Then a fresh and troubling thought crossed her mind. It was so disturbing that she halted in applying her lipstick to consider it. Could Carl have cleverly staged the whole thing? What if he had an accomplice and had arranged with that person to be waiting for them at the villa?

The blow Carl had received had not been a serious one at all. She was somewhat surprised that it had left him unconscious even briefly. Suppose Carl had instructed the accomplice to strike him, but to do as little harm as possible? The next step would be her discovering Carl on the floor, and then the "ghost's" attack on her. The climax, of course, had to be Carl's coming to the rescue and being made a hero in her eyes, while his accomplice vanished discreetly.

The dreadful thing about this scenario was that it all fitted within the realm of possibility. Trudy tried to dismiss the disturbing theory from her mind and went on with her makeup.

But the suspicion was there and could not be altogether erased from her thoughts. Her doubts about the handsome doctor were founded on the evidence of her own eyes. She had seen him with Sylvia in his arms. And Sylvia had postponed her return to New York and her husband.

Carl might still be determined to woo and win Trudy for his own reasons—reasons unknown to her but that could benefit him. Perhaps to help his employer get control of the villa. Carl might be the one named as her heir in Julia's will. If so, only she stood between him and the millions left to her.

She slipped on the black dress, which seemed best for the occasion. Its low neckline and single large panel of white made it attractively chic. Surveying herself in the full-length glass by the door, she was satisfied that her makeup had covered the first signs of black-and-blue on her throat. She'd planned to wear a white shawl if she hadn't been successful.

All her thinking was complicated by the fact that Carl, devious as he might be, appealed to her as a man. She could admit she'd almost been on the edge of losing her heart to him when she'd discovered him with Sylvia. Since then, it had been a struggle on her part to try to dismiss him as someone she could truly care for.

Even now her fears and concerns about the legacy her aunt had left her were surprisingly overshadowed by her grief that Carl had betrayed her. He had seemed so right, and she had felt he had the same feelings for her. Perhaps he did but was too committed to Sylvia to follow the honest dictates of his heart.

So she was still caught in the same trap of not knowing whom to trust. The face of Tom Clarendon came to her clearly. She knew she could depend on him. He was young, honest and a rebel. If he knew all the facts, he would not hesitate to try to protect her. Even Lena Morel, who had been Julia's friend, might encourage him to do so.

This thought made Trudy feel less isolated and hopeless. There was someone she could turn to if she had to. She made up her mind to see Tom again as soon as possible. The better friends they became, the better her chances of survival.

As she descended the stairs, she heard the voices of the others in the living room, where they usually gathered before dinner. Sylvia greeted her and gave her a peck on the cheek.

"You poor dear," she murmured. "What an ordeal for you!"

"Not my happiest moment," Trudy admitted with a wry smile as Sylvia led her over to a high-backed chair.

Benson Steiburn came up to her, his white beard bristling. "I cannot believe such a thing happened!" he said angrily.

Carl spoke from where he stood on the other side of the room. "You have me as a witness."

Sylvia went toward him and said with sympathy, "Carl might have been killed, as well."

Her father's face was dark with anger. "By the thief—or thieves! It can't have been anyone else. They've had a free run of the house since Pascal had it closed up. They must have looted everything of value."

Carl said, "Maybe Pascal is aware of it. Maybe these thieves are sharing the profits of the loot with him."

"I trust Pascal implicitly," was Benson Steiburn's comment to this. "He may be sloppy and he is lazy, but I do not think of him as a criminal."

"It's very likely this person who's playing the swordsman is working on his own," Sylvia said. "He has keys to some entry and he's been continuing the thefts."

Trudy was secretly amused by their speculations and wondered if they were meant to confuse her. She could not resist saying, "Perhaps none of you has the answer. Why couldn't it be the real ghost?"

The art collector stared at her. "Of course you're joking! Very courageous of you, under the circumstances."

"Not at all," she said, pretending seriousness. "Others have seen the ghost and been victims of it, so why not Carl and me?"

Carl smiled sourly. "You do have a point. We accept the legacy of the swordsman when it suits us and dismiss it when it doesn't."

"But you were both injured," Sylvia protested.

"Yes," Carl agreed. "And I think the ghost we met with today was of the flesh-and-blood variety."

"The big question is what to do about it," Benson Steiburn said.

"No use reporting the incident to the local police," Carl said. "We have tried that in other instances. They make out a long report and never refer to it again."

Trudy said, "I think the main thing that made the attack on us possible this afternoon was the fact that the house lights weren't working. If they had been on, our intruder would not have been so bold."

"That is sensible," her host said. "Carl, please contact Pascal and have him see that the electrical equipment is working and that the lights are turned on at the earliest moment."

"He's probably already left for Genoa," Trudy said.

"I can call him there," Carl told her, "and he can arrange for the work to be done here."

Sylvia showed her disgust. "He should have done it in the first place."

Steiburn sighed. "The man is sloppy and downright careless."

"I think he has also been remiss about my aunt Julia's will," Trudy said. "I find myself an interim heiress rather than a permanent one."

"Monstrous!" Steiburn waved his lighted cigar in renewed agitation. "What went on in Julia's head to have her make such an arrangement?"

"Do you think it's legal?" Trudy asked him.

"Carl said you've thought of turning the matter over to me."

"Pascal feels your lawyers could best deal with an appeal of the document."

"And you agree?"

"Yes."

"Tomorrow I will have my legal chief contact Pascal in Genoa. We'll put whatever staff is needed on it."

"Isn't that liable to be a lot of wasted effort, Father?" Sylvia asked.

Her father looked surprised. "Why do you say that?"

"We all know the senior Pascal was much different from Giuseppe. I suspect when he drew up a will, it was well executed with no weaknesses in it. So how can you hope to break it?"

Benson shrugged. "On the grounds that Julia was not fully sane at the time it was made. The terms of the document make no sense at all. Forcing this young woman to hold on to the villa whether she likes it or not is sheer madness."

"People will be sure to say you're fighting the case for Trudy for your own selfish reasons. You do want to get your hands on the villa."

Her father scowled. "I don't care what people say!"

Carl spoke up quickly, as if wishing to prevent any quarrel between the two of them. "There is something else about this second will that worries me more than anything. Pascal seems to think Adrian Romitelli is named the beneficiary."

"And he is an unscrupulous, dangerous person," Sylvia said.

Benson Steiburn waved a hand in anger. "The whole thing is monstrous! I can't think what got into Julia's head!"

"In spite of what happened today," Trudy told them, "the thing I want to do most is further explore the villa."

"You'll be able to do that when we get the electricity going," Carl said. "I'd stay away until then."

The others were in general agreement about this as the before-dinner conversation ended. Later that evening Trudy was delighted to receive a phone call from Tom Clarendon.

"How strange you should call! I've been thinking of calling you."

"Lovely," he said in his genial way.

"I'd like to go to the beach with you one day soon," she said.

"A warm and sunny day is predicted for tomorrow," he told her. "Why delay any further?"

"Sounds great. A nice change from gloomy old houses."

"You should stay away from such places—you're far too young and pretty."

"And you're too free with your flattery," she playfully reproached him.

"Only when I'm overawed by true beauty," he countered. "How about eleven? After we have our swim, you can shower and change at Lena's place, and we'll have lunch with her."

"I'll bring a bag with my clothes," she promised. "I'm really looking forward to this."

And she was. In spite of her traumatic day and her injured throat, she slept soundly that night. Nor was her sleep troubled by the dreams that had tormented her earlier. On this night she found herself dreaming about New York and her friend Gloria. She and Gloria went out on one of their shopping expeditions and met Carl along the way. The handsome man was especially friendly and after he'd moved on, Gloria confided that she thought he was a truly interesting male.

When Trudy awoke, she went over the dream in her mind and found herself wondering wryly why Tom hadn't appeared in the dream sequence as the desirable male. After all, it was he with whom she was going to spend a good part of the day, and her relaxed mood had made her sleep well and have only pleasant dreams. Pleasant dreams of another man, Carl Redman. How perverse the unconscious could be! she mused.

At breakfast, Sylvia asked her what her plans were for the day, suggesting that they take a drive somewhere.

"I'm sorry," Trudy said. "I've promised to meet Tom and go swimming in the ocean."

Sylvia's eyes twinkled. "He is very personable. It ought to be fun."

"His being a New Yorker helps. We can always talk about home."

The dark girl nodded. "I understand."

"Don't you ever miss New York and your husband?"

Sylvia blushed. "Of course. I'd be back there now, but he's on the West Coast on business."

"I see. So there's no point in going back now to be alone."

"Not when I can be here with Father."

Trudy asked no more questions. There had been no previous mention of Sylvia's husband being away on business. More than likely it was a pretense designed to make Sylvia's remaining in Italy seem more reasonable—a cover-up for her romance with Carl.

The day was beautiful, and she selected a stylish if skimpy crimson bikini. She knew that a number of European women and even a few American women appeared on the beach topless, but she felt her bikini was daring enough and gave her a certain air of elan. She packed a white dress and underthings in a small bag, then put on a colorful wraparound beach dress and a wide-brimmed straw hat.

Carl met her as she came down to wait for Tom. "You're not thinking of using the pool?" he asked in surprise.

"Last thing on my mind," she said. "You're more apt to be over there than I."

His eyebrows raised. "Why do you say that?"

"Just making conversation," she said lightly. Actually, she had meant his being at the pool with Sylvia.

"So you're going swimming in the ocean," Carl said.

"Yes. Tom is coming for me," she told him with a smile.

Carl's handsome face shadowed. "Watch yourself with him."

Surprised, she asked, "What do you mean?"

"I mean he's an excellent swimmer," Carl hedged. "He's at it all the time. Don't let him tire you out, and don't go beyond your depth."

"Thanks. I'll remember that. I forget that, as a medical man, you think of such things," she said, amused and sure he was just a little jealous.

"I try to be practical," he replied rather stiffly. "By the way, I've talked to Pascal. An electrician will arrive at the villa this afternoon to check on the lights. He should be able to get them working soon."

"That's great."

"Give my best to Clarendon," he told her, then went on to the room Benson Steiburn used as an office.

Tom arrived promptly in the rather shabby black sedan that Trudy knew belonged to Lena Morel. He opened the door for her and eyed her with approval. As he got behind the wheel again, he said, "We couldn't have a more perfect morning. During the main summer season it's often too hot. The beaches are a lot less crowded also. And I've found a small cove that hardly anyone else uses." In his swim trunks and loose overshirt, he looked very much the virile male.

As Tom had promised, the beach was small and deserted. He set up an umbrella for shade, and they stripped for the ocean.

"I go for something like that," he told her, openly admiring her bikini.

"You can buy these almost anywhere," she countered.

He shook his head. "No good without the package. That's what makes it."

She laughed and said, "Shall we go in?"

Tom took her by the hand, and they ran down to the water like two happy children. Trudy forgot all her cares in the sheer joy of the moment. They didn't halt at the water's edge but went straight on until the gentle waves lapped around their waists. Tom's skin was glistening with drops of water, and his hair was plastered down. Trudy felt the thrill of the cool yet comforting salt water as it caressed her.

"Sorry you came?" he asked, his even white teeth showing in his broad smile.

"It's much better than I'd hoped," she told him.

"No pool can match this," he said. "Let's try a few strokes." And he led the way, swimming strongly and gracefully out beyond her.

She waited for a moment, then began to swim after him. The buoyancy of the salt water made the swimming easier than it would be in a pool with ordinary water. She felt she could swim endlessly. But after several minutes she became somewhat breathless and decided to go back to shore.

She walked up the beach and stretched out on the blanket Tom had placed under the umbrella. A few minutes later Tom came running up and threw himself down beside her. They toweled each other off, making a game out of it. Then they lay beside each other in complete relaxation, enjoying the sun's warmth.

"Why didn't Lena come along?" she asked.

"She has a slight headache," he said. "But she always gets over them by noon. She'll be fine by the time we arrive."

"She's an excellent swimmer, isn't she?"

"She is. And that's exciting in a woman of her age. But then she is a remarkable person in almost every way."

Trudy was tempted to query him about Lena's acting career these days but felt it might be better to avoid that subject. Instead, she lazily watched the sea gulls as they swooped in the air above her, crying hoarsely.

Tom broke the silence by saying, "I hear the will was read yesterday."

She leaned up on an elbow. "How did you know that?"

His hands behind his head, he smiled up at her. "It's a small place. News gets around. Romitelli saw you driving to Pascal's office in Carl's convertible. That could've been for only one thing."

"Leave it to Adrian," she said.

"Was everything in order?" he asked.

She decided to be wary about offering information concerning the interim legacy, at least until Benson Steiburn had time to consult his lawyers about appealing the will. So she merely said, "It was very much as I'd expected."

"Good," the young writer said. "Do you think you'll live in the villa?"

"I might."

"It's not exactly a fun place," Tom said. "Have you seen it from the inside?"

"Only briefly." She'd also made up her mind not to spread the news of the attack on her and Carl.

In view of this, it startled her to hear Tom ask jokingly, "Aren't you afraid of being alone in that old place? You know, legend has it that the ghost moves freely from Castle Malice to the villa and back. It's been seen in both places. Lena's cottage is newer and relatively safe from the unhappy spirit."

"I'm not sure I even take the legend seriously," she said.

"Better give it a second thought," he warned her. "Most of the locals swear the ghost exists. And Lena hints she saw something at the swimming pool when your aunt met her death."

Trudy glanced at him and said, "I believe we have a murderer here. And that he is pretending to be the masked swordsman and is using the legend for his own benefit."

This made Tom sit up. "*Who?*"

"I don't know," she admitted. "It could be one of Aunt Julia's former servants who stole from the villa while pretending to be the ghost."

"Interesting idea," he said. "In fact, it makes very good sense."

"Whoever it is, I think he was responsible for my aunt's drowning."

"You don't accept it was an accident?"

"Does Lena Morel truly believe it was?"

Tom looked embarrassed. "The truth is, she was very drunk that night and remembers it all only vaguely."

"So it could have been a murder rather than an accidental drowning," she said, gazing at him earnestly.

Tom smiled sadly. "Here we have the sun, the beach, the ocean and each other, yet all we can talk about is murder." And without giving her a chance for a reply, he took her in his arms and kissed her hungrily. At first she was startled by his hasty approach, but as the seconds passed, the feel of his arms around her and his lips caressing hers seemed all the more natural and desirable.

CHAPTER TEN

WHEN TOM RELEASED HER he still held on to her hands as he gazed at her earnestly. "I hope you understand that wasn't an attempt at a quick conquest. I really care for you."

Trudy smiled ruefully. "Under the circumstances, I'm glad."

"I'm not good at heroic gestures," he went on. "I usually do things clumsily. So my approach was sudden rather than tender. It's all that I'm capable of."

The good-looking young man showed a boyish sincerity that she found impossible to doubt. "I like your honesty, Tom. It is rare."

"And I like your directness and your goodness. As if that weren't enough, you're also lovely!"

"I'm sure you'll find many flaws in me when you come to know me better."

"I thought maybe you were interested in Carl Redman and wouldn't want to look at another man."

"Why should you think that?"

"The way he looks at you—the attention he's paid you since your arrival."

"I think Carl does that automatically. He makes a habit of being charming to any female within his orbit."

"You know he wanted to marry Sylvia and that she changed her mind about the match."

Trudy nodded. "I've heard the story from every viewpoint."

"They still seem to be good friends," Tom said.

"Yes, they do," she agreed. "And I hope we can also become good friends. I sometimes feel terribly alone here."

He squeezed her hand. "Depend on it," he told her.

"Now I think we should try the water again and then go on to Lena's. She'll be wondering what happened to us."

"Right you are!"

Their second time in the water was almost as enjoyable but they didn't remain in it as long. After they came out and were toweling off before going to the car, Tom pointed toward the horizon.

"Straight out there, a good distance away, there is a raft anchored. It's for long-distance swimmers who need to rest before returning to shore. I've gone out there on good days. It's an exciting experience, and I'd like to share it with you some time."

"I'm not sure I could make it," she said, gazing out at the raft.

"It's easy enough when the water is really calm," he assured her. "Even a modest swimmer can manage it."

She laughed as she put on her beach dress. "Well, I'm certainly modest when it comes to my swimming talent."

"You do okay," he said, picking up the blanket and the beach umbrella. "We must come here more often. It's been a lot of fun."

LENA MOREL, looking less tense than usual, greeted
them at her door in a stylish dress of rainbow-colored
whirls against a black background. She smilingly announced that her headache was over and sent Trudy to
the bathroom off her bedroom to shower and change.

Trudy showered as quickly as she could. She was
elated to be accepted by these two people as friends.
They provided the safety valve she needed to with-
stand the stress she was going through and of which
there seemed no end in sight. Tom's lovemaking at the
beach had been so boyish and sincere she couldn't feel
he'd been trying to take advantage of her.

Actually, she'd wanted to establish a close bond
with the writer. Not that she wished they would become lovers; rather, she hoped they could become
good friends. She was pleased that Lena Morel seemed
to be actively interested in seeing that she and Tom
became closer. According to Tom, Lena had no illu-
sions about her age, nor any jealousy regarding him.
They were business partners in a project that could
bring them both money and some fame if they were
successful.

As Trudy made some final adjustments to her dress,
she noticed the many framed photos on the walls of
the film star's bedroom. Her curiosity caused her to
take the time to study a few of them. Most had been
taken on movie sets with the famous Hollywood leading men Lena had worked with over the years. Lena
looked so much younger and radiant in these photos,
it was no wonder she could only get small supporting
roles in movies made for television.

Lena had prepared shrimp salad for lunch, and after drinking a glass of wine, they all sat down to it. The

former star showed a friendly interest in their doings at the beach without being too inquisitive.

As they lingered over coffee, Tom, now in a white shirt and fawn slacks, smiled across the table at Lena and said, "Romitelli was right. They did have the reading of the will yesterday."

Lena looked at Trudy. "So it is settled."

"In a sense," she said carefully. "There are still some things to be looked into."

Tom nodded. "It always takes a while to thrash out all the fine print. But at least you know you're Julia's heir."

"Yes," she said.

"I'm glad to hear that," the actress said. "You know, right up until now I've been worried... because of something Julia said to me."

Trudy was at once curious. "What did she say?"

Lena smiled in apology. "It doesn't matter now, since the will has been read and you know where you stand. But I asked her about Romitelli. I knew he'd been depending on her for most of his living expenses. So I asked her if she had made any provision for him in the event she died suddenly."

"What did she say?" Trudy asked, more curious than ever.

Lena grimaced. "She hated to think of death or dying. She talked all around my question. But finally she told me not to worry, that she had provided handsomely for him."

"Was there anything of this in the will?" Tom asked Trudy.

"No," she said. "But in the event of my death, there is a second will."

Lena Morel and the young writer both seemed surprised to hear this. "Isn't that unusual?" Lena asked.

"It may not even be legal," Trudy told her. "Mr. Steiburn is looking into it now."

Tom frowned. "His lawyers should soon find out whatever there is to know. But I'm afraid I have the opinion that the will is valid if properly drawn."

Lena was incredulous. "This makes you an heiress only for your lifetime. After that everything goes to the person named in that will!"

"Yes," Trudy said, hoping she hadn't made a grave error by revealing this much to them.

Tom gave her a glance filled with alarm. "From what Julia said to Lena, it's almost certain Adrian Romitelli will be the heir to succeed you."

She nodded. "I think there's a strong possibility of that."

Lena Morel looked angry. "We were all good friends to Julia. Yet she picked someone who was not particularly loyal to her. I don't understand it."

"I don't understand her treatment of Trudy," Tom said with indignation. "Not only is she not going to be the sole heir, but she will have to live under the shadow of someone like Romitelli standing by, ready to gain by her death."

Lena seemed troubled at the mere mention of this. "Let us hope we are wrong."

Tom complained, "No matter how you look at it, there's no question that it's an unhappy situation."

"That is why Mr. Steiburn wants to help me," Trudy said.

Lena and Tom exchanged glances, and then the actress said, "My dear, Benson Steiburn is one of my friends. But I must warn you, he is ruthless when anything stands in his way. And it is well known that he wants to get his hands on the villa property.''

Tom nodded. ''No wonder he wants to break the will. Unless he does, you cannot sell it to him.''

''I'm not at all sure I would in any case,'' Trudy said defensively.

''Just be cautious in what you do and say,'' Lena told her. ''Neither Tom nor I have anything to gain from you. Believe that we are your friends, and you may come to us for help at any time.''

Tom agreed. ''Yes. Please remember that.''

''I'm truly grateful,'' Trudy said. ''I'd hoped I'd be able to depend on you two. Everything is so strange to me here. And now the news about a second will makes me wish I had never made the journey.''

The young writer got up impulsively and came over to her. ''Please don't say that, Trudy. Otherwise we'd never have met.''

Lena smiled tolerantly. ''Tom finds you attractive. And so do I.''

''I really must be getting back,'' Trudy said, rising. ''Thank you for the lovely lunch.''

Lena saw her to the door. ''We will do it again and often.''

Tom drove her back to Castle Malice. When she invited him to come in, he refused. ''Sorry. I've got some work to do on the book. Another time.''

''I enjoyed the beach and the lunch very much,'' she said with a smile.

''We'll do it soon again,'' he promised. ''I'll call you.''

They parted good friends, as she had hoped. It made her less apprehensive to know she had Lena and the young writer to turn to if things became threatening at Castle Malice. At first she'd felt that Carl would be the one whom she could depend on, but that had changed when she'd discovered him and Sylvia together.

She entered the castle and was heading for the stairway when Benson Steiburn called out her name and came over to her. The older man seemed to be in a good mood.

"I've been in touch with my lawyers in Genoa," he said, "and they will be talking to Pascal about the will."

"Thank you."

He eyed her closely. "Did you have a pleasant day at the beach?"

"Yes, I really enjoyed it."

"Good." Steiburn stroked his beard for a moment, then said, "One other thing. The electricians were over at the villa this afternoon. They will have the power on tomorrow."

Trudy smiled. "Then I can give the place a closer look."

"But not by yourself. After what has been happening, you must show extreme caution. You do understand that?"

"I do," she said. "Probably Carl or someone else will go through the villa with me. I won't feel so much in danger with the lights on."

"The unfortunate thing about these old houses," Benson Steiburn went on, "is that they are like sieves as far as security is concerned. There are so many possible ways of entry—some of them secret, like the tunnel connecting us to the villa—that it is next to impossible to keep out anyone who's determined to create mischief."

"I realize the hazards," she told him.

"Happily, we all sleep in the same wing, so we are close to one another if there should be a problem in the night. A single cry should awaken at least one of us."

She smiled bleakly. "Yes. I found that out the night when I saw the death mask on my pillow."

Anger showed suddenly on his face. "I'm still trying to get to the bottom of that! Whoever took that mask and placed it there should be dealt with harshly."

"It was meant to scare me away."

"I admire your courage," he said. "And rest assured that I will do something to have that unfair will changed."

She went upstairs and rested for a while. When it was time to go down for dinner, she put on her yellow dress and went out on the balcony for a moment to enjoy the evening air. It was still pleasantly warm, and she had a broad view of the gardens. Then she saw Sylvia and Carl, strolling arm in arm in a distant part of the garden. All the suspicions she'd had about them earlier were now confirmed.

By the time she went downstairs, they had returned and were awaiting her with Benson Steiburn. Sylvia came up to her and said, "We have decided on a wonderful way to entertain you!"

Trudy replied with a discreet "Really?"

Sylvia turned to Carl and instructed him, "You tell her! You're able to explain it better."

Carl smiled and took a step toward Trudy. "Did you know that Palina has a wine festival every year?"

"No," she said. "I didn't."

Benson Steiburn chuckled. "Nor would you be expected to."

Carl went on. "It lasts for a week. Mostly, the village people take part in the various events, but they welcome those of us who have made the area our second home. The gala night of the festival is a costume ball."

"And that is tomorrow night!" Sylvia said, smiling happily.

"We have decided to attend," Carl said, "and we want you to come along."

Trudy turned to her host and asked, "Are you going, Mr. Steiburn?"

He shook his head. "I'm too old for such revelry. But I think you and Sylvia should enjoy it. If Carl is willing to escort you, I'm sure you'll be safe."

Carl gave her a pleading, good-humored look. "Sylvia was the one who suggested it. I think it would be great fun for you. We needn't stay long."

"Where is this costume ball held?" Trudy asked, feeling that she was probably being used so that Carl and Sylvia could go to the affair without upsetting Sylvia's father.

"It's held on the common in front of the town hall. All the buildings are lit up and decorated with lanterns. Wine is freely dispensed, and drinking and dancing go hand in hand. At the end of the evening, when the village trio you heard here has finished playing, a prize is given for the best male and female costumes."

"Then we all have to wear costumes?" Trudy asked.

"That's easy," Sylvia told her. "We can make them from things we have."

"I always attend as a clown," Carl confessed with a laugh. "It's a costume I once used to entertain at a children's party long ago. I've kept it and worn it ever since."

"It sounds like fun," Trudy said, "though I can't think of any costume."

"I can," Sylvia declared. "You can go as Little Red Riding Hood. I'll let you have my red cape with a hood. All you'll need is a mask and a basket to carry."

"What will you be?" Trudy wanted to know.

"The Queen of Hearts," Sylvia said. "Father bought me the outfit years ago. I looked at it this afternoon and it's still in good shape."

Benson Steiburn said, "It's a jolly affair. You should go."

Trudy felt she could not refuse and decided it might be an amusing evening. "I'd enjoy seeing more of the local people."

"Nearly everyone will be there," Carl promised. "Including many from the foreign colony like ourselves."

So it was decided that they would attend the village celebration. Dinner proved uneventful, but the mood changed when it was over and an unexpected guest arrived in the person of Adrian Romitelli.

The pinch-faced man looked a trifle less dejected than usual as he joined them in the living room. Steiburn greeted him in a friendly fashion.

At once Romitelli questioned Sylvia. "Are you planning to attend the gala this year?"

Sylvia nodded. "Yes. We've been discussing costumes. Trudy wants to see everything that goes on."

"It is a fine affair," Adrian said in his precise way. "What costume are you wearing, Trudy?"

"Sylvia suggested I go as Little Red Riding Hood," she told him.

"What do you think of that?" Carl was clearly flattering the man by asking his opinion.

Adrian considered, then replied, "I think that's a good idea." Turning to Trudy again, he said, "The main thing is that you don't miss it. You can attend in ordinary clothes, if you like. None of the villagers would mind."

"It's more fun to dress up," Carl said.

"I shall be going as a monk in a black robe," Adrian informed them.

Sylvia protested. "But others use that same disguise! You should wear something more original!"

"I have the costume, and I intend to use it."

"So what if there will be a half-dozen monks at the party? Who cares?" Carl said cheerfully.

Romitelli gave him a scathing look and then directed his attentions to Sylvia, taking her aside and seating himself beside her on a sofa as he told her at length of a recent tennis tournament he had won in Lerici.

Benson Steiburn had made a discreet retreat to the library, so Carl took Trudy by the arm and led her out into the gardens.

"I had to rescue you from that bore," he said as they stood there under the stars.

"What about Sylvia?" she asked, smiling.

Against the background of the blue-tinted night shadows, Carl looked more handsome than ever. It was one of those moments when Trudy almost felt she could forgive him for his deception.

"Sylvia has a gift for turning people off. She can appear to be listening when she's hearing nothing at all. She simply smiles and looks attentive."

"I must try and cultivate that," Trudy said.

He was studying her closely. "How did your day at the beach go?"

"It was great fun!"

"Tom Clarendon is a good swimmer, and so is Lena," he remarked.

"She wasn't there."

He raised his eyebrows. "Just the two of you? How cozy."

"We went in the water twice and then we joined Lena for lunch. I hope that meets with your approval."

"I didn't mean to show disapproval. I'm sorry. I have no right to."

"I'm glad you realize that."

"But don't let Tom's boyish charm fool you. I've heard a couple of peculiar stories about him."

"Peculiar?"

"He was mixed up with a group that organized a fake real-estate deal in Rome. He was the public-relations man. A few of the primary offenders went to jail, but Tom and several minor officials got off."

"How do you know he was part of the swindle?" she asked. "He may have thought he was working for honest employers."

"I'd find that extremely difficult to believe."

"Lena must think he's honest. She chose him to do her book."

Carl smiled grimly. "She's as desperate for money as he is. They make a good pair."

"I think you're being cruel, Carl, trying to spoil the fun I had this afternoon!"

He touched her arm placatingly, but she drew away from him. "Please, Trudy, don't misunderstand!"

"The trouble is, I understand too well."

"I don't know what you're talking about," he said. "But I know I'm simply trying to warn you against those two. They're neither naive nor innocent."

Trudy's smile was derisive. "There seems to be a shortage of innocence here."

"The baleful influence of Castle Malice," he told her.

"I'm afraid I must agree with you on that," she said.

His expression was mocking as he asked, "Does it cheer you to have Romitelli, your probable heir apparent, around?"

Before she could make a reply to this, Sylvia came out with Adrian in tow. "I've just heard the most thrilling account of Adrian's last tournament. He won by three games!"

"Two," Adrian said. "I don't believe you were listening to me, Sylvia."

"Oh, but I was," Sylvia said with wide-eyed innocence.

"Never mind," Carl said. "We're all going to have fun at the costume ball tomorrow night."

Adrian gave Trudy a sad glance. "I was there with Julia last year. She wore a Mother Goose costume, and everyone complimented her on it. Who could have predicted then what was to happen?''

"I'm sure you miss her," Trudy said.

"You can hardly guess how much," was his doleful reply. "We spent so much time in each other's company."

Sylvia nodded. "That's true. I can't think of anyone who was closer to her than you."

Romitelli's face became blotched with anger. "Lena Morel pretends she was the one who knew her best. Pure rot! It was she who let poor Julia drown because she was too drunk to go help her."

"Unless you were there that night, you can hardly make a statement like that," Trudy reproached him.

"I wasn't there," he snapped. "It's common knowledge she's drunk by nine almost every night."

Sylvia sighed heavily. "We all know you cared for Julia and how bad you feel about her death. But we don't want to hear these personal attacks against Lena Morel."

Romitelli was the one who apparently was not listening now. Staring mournfully off into space, he said, "She's tried to reach me. Tried to give me a message."

"What sort of message?" Carl asked.

"A personal thing between us. Do you remember that her favorite perfume had a strong scent of wild violets?"

"Yes, I do remember," Sylvia said. "It was expensive. She had it sent from Rome."

"I often told her how much it suited her. She liked that."

"What has all that got to do with her trying to send you a message from the other side of the grave?" Carl demanded.

"This will interest you, Trudy," Adrian said with an unusual note of familiarity.

"In what way?" she asked.

"It will show you what a strong person Julia was. I was very depressed the other night. I woke up in the early-morning hours with the darkness still around me, and my bedroom was filled with the fragrance of wild violets."

Sylvia said in a hushed voice, "Her perfume."

"I got up and turned on the light. There was no one in the room, yet the fragrance of wild violets lingered. *Her* fragrance."

"Is this supposed to be some sort of ghost story?" Carl asked brusquely. "I doubt that Trudy appreciates it."

"I don't mind," she said. "Please go on."

Romitelli nodded. "I went back to bed. In the morning I decided I'd had a bad dream. The aroma of wild violets was gone. But as I crossed the room to take a shower, I saw something that made me halt."

Trudy could not help but be fascinated by Adrian's strange story. "What?" she asked.

His eyes met hers. "It was a handkerchief, a tiny handkerchief with Julia's initials. The scent of wild violets was there as I touched it to my nostrils. I had never seen such a handkerchief before—nor did I own anything like it. So I knew it was the message I'd been longing for...the message from Julia."

CHAPTER ELEVEN

THERE WAS A LONG MOMENT of embarrassed silence after Adrian finished his story. No one was sure what sort of comment to make. Carl was frowning, and Sylvia looked stunned. Trudy guessed that her own face must register something of the same amazement. Adrian continued to wear an expression of smug satisfaction.

Trudy felt she must somehow ease the awkward situation, so she summoned a small smile and said, "It seems to me you must have had a lady visitor who used that same perfume."

Adrian shook his head. "No. It was Julia who came to me. I'm certain of that. And I understood her message."

Carl stared at him and spoke in a voice that barely concealed his annoyance. "What was the message?"

Adrian's smile was cold. "I do not intend to share it with you now. But you will all know it in good time."

His obvious smugness and his smile at once suggested to Trudy that the information she'd gained from Giuseppe Pascal must be correct. Adrian was indeed the person named as heir in her aunt's second will.

Sylvia said rather irritably, "I think it was stupid to lead us on that way and then refuse to explain anything."

Romitelli remained calm and self-assured. "You would not understand in any case," he told her. Then he turned to Trudy and asked, "Will you join me for tennis tomorrow at ten?"

She hesitated, then decided she should accept. Perhaps he intended to tell her something he was keeping from the others. "I'll be ready," she said.

He looked pleased. "I'll come by for you," he promised.

Then Carl saw him out, leaving Trudy and Sylvia alone on the patio.

"Did you ever hear anything as wild as that?" Sylvia wanted to know, shuddering slightly.

Trudy shrugged. "He seemed convinced he had a ghostly visitation."

"Either he's a little mad, or someone played a practical joke on him!"

"To play that kind of joke, you'd have to have a macabre sense of humor. But then there was that death mask left on the pillow beside me."

Sylvia's shapely brows lifted. "You think the two incidents might be linked?"

"It makes one wonder."

"I must tell Father about this," Sylvia said in a troubled voice. "Let's go inside."

They entered the hallway just in time to meet Carl, on his way back from seeing Adrian off. The doctor gave them a grim smile and said, "Wasn't that something!"

"Trudy thinks the handkerchief and some of the other weird happenings may be linked."

Carl nodded. "I wouldn't be surprised."

Trudy was surprised he agreed so readily. "You think it's possible?"

"I'd say probable. And I'd also say the man behind everything is Romitelli himself. He told us that story about the violet-scented handkerchief to throw us off the track."

"An interesting theory," Trudy said, though she was not all that sure she agreed with him.

"And you are going to play tennis with him again?" Carl asked.

"Why not? It could be enlightening."

Carl looked skeptical. "It might also be an ordeal. You know how he is about winning."

"I understand him now," she said. "I think I can handle it."

Sylvia stifled a yawn. "It's getting late, and we'll be up until all hours tomorrow night. Let's call it a day."

Upstairs in her room, Trudy did not find sleep at once. She lay in bed staring into the darkness and wondering what the key to the puzzle might be. She felt certain that all the strange events were part of some diabolical scheme. In all probability, a scheme to eliminate her.

She wanted to depend on Carl, but the strong doubts concerning his relationship with Sylvia still remained. Even Sylvia's father was concerned about her lack of plans to return to New York. It all appeared to add up to an affair between Carl and Sylvia, no matter how vigorously he had denied this.

Under these circumstances, Trudy felt her best friend might well be Tom Clarendon. She had enjoyed the time at the beach with him and had not found his embrace unpleasant. It would be to Tom she would look for help and guidance. She believed Carl's comments about the newspaperman's dubious past activities had been no more than a deliberate smear campaign to turn her against him.

Her thoughts focused next on Adrian Romitelli. Was he really the heir named in the second will, as well as the person who was doing all these frightening things to terrify her? She hoped to be able to size him up better when they faced each other on the tennis court in the morning. That had been her only reason for accepting his invitation.

Finally, she slept. But it was a sleep filled with gliding phantoms and abrupt appearances of the masked swordsman from out of dark shadows. She moaned and tossed restlessly as the nightmares tormented her.

Early the next morning Sylvia thoughtfully brought a fresh tennis outfit to her, so she was dressed and ready by ten. As she waited for Adrian to arrive, she strolled across the grounds to study the villa that was part of her legacy, then halted by the swimming pool. It continued to have a sinister air about it.

There was a footstep behind her, and she turned quickly to see Carl approaching. He smiled bleakly and asked, "Do you have a morbid fascination for that pool?"

"It does seem to draw me," she admitted.

"I'd try and stay away from it," he advised. "I think that's best for you."

"Why?" she asked.

He indicated the villa and its grounds with a wave of his hand. "All this represents something dark and unhappy, as far as I'm concerned. I think you should sell it, let it be torn down and so set the ghost at rest."

"I doubt that the ghost I'm fighting can be disposed of that easily. And the way the will stands now, I can't put the villa up for sale."

"Let Benson Steiburn look after that," Carl urged her. "His lawyers can always find loopholes in any agreement." He hesitated and then said rather awkwardly, "By the way, if you decide to sell the villa's art collection as a lot, I'd like to handle it for you. I have contacts with some of the best dealers in Italy, as well as all over the world. I think I can honestly say I could do better for you than anyone else."

This sudden offer caught Trudy by surprise. "I'll surely think about it. I suppose you know Aunt Julia's collection better than most people."

"I do. In fact, I was the purchasing agent for quite a few of her paintings and some of the other art objects."

"I want to go through the house again, with the lights working," she said. "No more experiences like the last time."

"We can do that very soon," he assured her. Then he looked over her shoulder and winced. "Here comes your tennis partner. If you'll excuse me, I'm going back to the castle now." He turned and hurried off.

Trudy was mildly amused at his not wanting to face Adrian. She was also still surprised by his almost pressing request to be given permission to sell the villa's art collection.

Romitelli came up to her with an annoyed expression on his face. "Am I so repulsive to Carl that he has to run away from me?"

"He had to get back," she said, trying to smooth things over. "He said he was expecting a phone call."

"I'm sure it must have been urgent." Adrian's sour tone belied his words.

She held up her racket and smiled at him. "Let's go right to the courts."

He lost some of his anger during their walk but said nothing about Julia. The court they had used before was free, and he chose it; evidently it was a favorite of his. They volleyed for a little while and then began the first game.

Trudy was startled to realize Adrian was not playing as seriously as he had on their previous encounter. He was not as aggressive in his serve, and she was able to make some points she'd otherwise have lost. It amazed her that he was so much more relaxed today.

The outcome was that she won a set. This was more than she'd hoped for, and she couldn't help feeling he had deliberately held himself back.

As they left the court, she said, "You were too kind to me."

"You played well," he said simply. "Let's go somewhere and sit down for a while."

"If you like," she said, wondering what he might have to say.

On the broad lawn by the tennis courts there were several wrought-iron tables and chairs, all painted white. He led her to one of the round tables, and they sat down.

Looking around, he observed, "Plenty of privacy here." He placed his racket on an empty chair next to her and stared at her silently for a moment.

"What did Redman have to say this morning?" was his first question.

His directness startled her. She spread her hands in a vague gesture. "Not much. We talked about my selling the villa, and he said he'd like to handle the sale of the art collection if I sold the building."

Adrian looked grimly amused. "That sounds like him. He bought many of those paintings for your aunt and made a nice, fat commission on them. Now he wants to get another one from you."

"He said he thought he could do better for me than anyone else," she ventured.

The eyes of the man in the chair opposite her flashed angrily. "Don't believe him!" Adrian snapped. "If you decide to sell the paintings, at least talk to some of the other dealers. Don't sell yourself short!"

"Are you saying that Carl might cheat me?"

"Yes, I am." Adrian leaned close to her and continued. "He's been cheating Steiburn for years. Sylvia is in love with him, so she helps cover up his behavior."

Trudy knew that Adrian disliked almost all the cliffside inhabitants, but she was shocked to hear him make these direct accusations. "It's dangerous to say such things unless you are certain of their truth."

"Things speak for themselves," he grunted. "Sylvia was supposed to return to her husband weeks ago. Instead, she stays here—to be with Carl Redman!"

Even though Trudy believed the same thing, she was not ready to admit it, especially not to Adrian. "As a guest of Mr. Steiburn's, I feel I should not discuss the matter."

He sat back in his chair and laughed harshly. "And you are also in love with him, aren't you?"

"Please!" she said, embarrassed and angry, and started to stand up.

"I apologize," he said quickly in a placating tone and eased her back into her chair. "I only wish to help you, not offend you."

"If you have nothing more to say, I think I should be leaving," she told him coldly.

His face showed the smug expression so familiar to him. "You dislike me as much as the others do. You just cover it up better."

"I *don't* like the way you've been talking!"

"Sorry," he said. "For your benefit, believe me. And I'll tell you something else. I was closer to Julia than anyone guesses. She confided in me whose name is in that second will—the name of the person who inherits everything in the event of your death."

This was what she had hoped he might say. Her nerves on edge, she asked, "Whose name is it?"

He chuckled. "Come, now, that information is my provision for my old age."

"You mean you want to sell it?"

"I intend to sell it," he said confidently. "Are you interested in being the highest bidder?"

"I think not," she said. "For I believe you are the person named in that will."

His smile was cryptic. "You heard that from that fat fool Pascal."

"Where I heard it is not important," she said. "Is it true?"

He smiled smugly. "It will cost you a pretty penny to find out. You should thank me for making you the offer of the information."

"I won't be blackmailed!" she said, rising.

"Such an ugly word." Romitelli was also on his feet now.

"That's what you're attempting to do."

"I'll not argue the point. I will only tell you I was a good friend of Julia's. I'm trying to be the same sort of friend to you. Think about my offer, and above all else, don't mention it to anyone."

"I'm not sure I can promise you that."

He seized her arm so tightly that she winced. "If you have any brains at all, my girl, you'll know that loose talk about this subject will place us both in danger. Do you understand?"

"Let me go!" she cried, trying to pull away from him.

His eyes had a fanatical gleam as they fixed on hers. "You will say nothing!"

"All right," she gasped, not caring as long as he let her go. Immediately he relaxed his painful grip on her arm, and she stumbled back.

"When we are with the others, you will behave toward me with the usual courtesy." And with that he bowed and marched away, leaving her to stare after him with stricken eyes.

She stood in the warm sunlight, massaging her arm where he'd hurt it and thinking about what he'd said. She decided he might be right; better not to say anything yet. But she was sure beyond a doubt that he was the other heir.

Trudy walked slowly back to the castle. Seated in the garden was Benson Steiburn. On seeing her, he put down the newspaper he had been reading and asked, "Did you have a good game?"

She managed a smile. "I won a set."

"You must have been in good form," the older man said. Then he frowned slightly. "Perhaps you exerted yourself too much. You're terribly pale."

"It was a taxing contest," she admitted. "I'll feel better after I have a shower."

"One thing before you go. Tom came by to see you."

"I'm sorry I missed him," she said, brightening at the mention of his name.

"He wanted to talk to you about the costume party tonight," Steiburn continued amiably. "He and Lena Morel are going, of course. I told him all you young people here planned to attend."

"I wonder what he and Lena are wearing."

"I have no idea. But he seemed very pleased to know that you'd be attending. He'll no doubt watch out for you."

"I'm sure we'll meet," she agreed.

"By the way, the power in the villa is working now. I had my maintenance man test it earlier this morning. So you will have lights whenever you wish to inspect the place again."

"Thank you," she said. "Since it has gone so long already, I'll probably wait another day."

Trudy showered and had a light lunch, then took a short nap later in the afternoon. She was sorry she had missed Tom, because it occurred to her that he was perhaps the only one to whom she'd dare reveal the things that Adrian had said to her. He was the only one she could truly trust.

At the dinner table there was much revelry as the wine festival was discussed. Everyone had stories to tell of the fun and excitement of previous festivals. Trudy listened and couldn't help thinking that last year at this time her aunt had been a happy participant, and now she was dead. Could the same thing happen to her?

Finally Sylvia announced, "It is time to dress. We must all parade our costumes before my father."

Carl laughed. "That's the custom!"

Benson Steiburn looked pleased. "I'm delighted to be included to this extent. When you are ready, do come down."

On the way upstairs Carl told Trudy, "You heard that Romitelli is coming as a monk. There will be a dozen dressed like him. He's so obstinate he won't change his mind even when he knows he's making a mistake. How did your tennis game go?" This last was said in a rush.

"Not bad," she said, grateful that she was now at the door of her room and did not have to discuss it any further.

Her costume was simple. It consisted of a voluminous white skirt, a white blouse and a wide red sash. After she put it on, she placed Sylvia's sweeping red cape over her shoulders and tucked the hood over her head to partially cover her blond hair. Then she slipped on her mask. Studying herself in the mirror, she felt it was not a terribly original costume but that it would do.

There was the sound of laughter outside her door and then a knock on it. After she opened the door, a lavishly dressed eighteenth-century lady and a colorful clown came bouncing in. Sylvia whirled in her finery and curtsied to Trudy.

"You look marvelous! You truly do!" Trudy declared.

Carl had whitened his face and painted his nose a rosy red; bright red spots dotted his cheeks. His clown costume was in the usual tradition of red, white and blue, and his hat was a cone of red. In his right hand he held a white ball suspended by some kind of elastic band. He swung the ball at Trudy and then laughed as it jerked back to him when the elastic took effect.

"Don't neglect me," he implored, kneeling before her.

She was laughing, too. "You both look so great! I feel like a pale shadow beside you."

"You look very well," Sylvia said, throwing an arm around her. "Now let's go downstairs and have Father report on us."

A few moments later they were in the big living room, parading before Benson Steiburn. The older man applauded them heartily. "I vow there won't be any better costumes at the ball," was his opinion.

They went outside to the car and headed for the village. As they drove through the dark night, Trudy once again felt a surge of nervous apprehension about the night ahead. There was no reason for this that she could think of, so she assumed it was merely a black mood on her part. Not wanting to put a damper on the party, she attempted to ignore the small nagging within her.

Carl parked the white convertible on a side street. The three of them linked arms, with Carl in the middle, and walked along the cobblestoned streets to the lighted area fronting the common. The village band was playing, and many of the hundreds of people gathered were doing a country dance.

"Did we exaggerate?" Carl asked Trudy.

"No," she said, staring at the colorful lights and the people enjoying the music. "It's wonderful!"

"You see, everyone is masked and in costume," Sylvia pointed out.

"First we must have some wine," Carl told them. "The wine is free and generously served." Soon they were lined up at the wine bar and, as their turns came, were handed great goblets of either white or red wine.

Trudy stared at the goblet of white wine in her hand. "I can never drink all of this!" she exclaimed.

But no one heard her, because no one was listening to her. The din of voices and loud music continued, and she stood on the sidelines, sipping her wine. Then, all at once, she saw that Carl and Sylvia had joined the dancers. How like them, she thought, to go off and leave her so they could be together in the midst of all the festivities.

She felt lonely and hurt. Tears stung her eyes, and she was about to turn away when a masked man in a monk's costume came up to her. He bowed ceremoniously, took the wine goblet from her hand, then seized her in his arms and danced off with her. Soon they were in the middle of the laughing crowd of dancers.

Trudy was breathless as her lively partner whirled her around. She tried to study his features, but the mask and the monk's cowl concealed his identity. Then she recalled that Adrian was coming as a monk, and she knew at once who her partner was.

"Adrian!" she cried, not expecting him to hear her.

If he did, he made no sign of it. He kept whirling her around so that she was rapidly becoming dizzy as well as out of breath. The dance seemed endless. Then she sensed that they were gradually moving to the outer ring of dancers, and she felt some hope. Her partner swung her about as before, but suddenly he danced away from the outer circle and down a narrow cobblestoned alley. Then he halted and held her by the hands.

The sound of the music still reached them, as did the glow of light all around the common. Trudy stood there for a moment before she managed to say, "It is you, Adrian!"

The monk continued to hold her hands, and a soft, mirthless laugh emerged from under the cowl. The laugh was so menacing it sent an icy chill down her spine.

"Adrian! Speak to me!" she begged him and tried to pull away.

The monk released her hands but stood directly in her path, so that there was no escape up the small alley to where the crowd was assembled. Trudy realized she was trapped.

Then, very slowly, the man lifted his cowl. Facing her was not Adrian Romitelli, but the sinister figure of the masked swordsman!

"No!" she screamed and turned and fled down the dark alley.

As she stumbled along, sobbing, she heard him close on her heels. She fought bravely to go on, but all at once she came to a wooden barrier. The alley was a dead end! She let out a wail of despair, her fingers scraping the rotting, wet wood as she collapsed against it and slid to the ground.

CHAPTER TWELVE

TRUDY GROANED AND STIRRED a little, vaguely aware of loud voices clamoring at her. Then she opened her eyes to find herself blinded by a bright light thrust close to her face. She gave a small moan of protest as she tried to fend the light off.

"Are you all right, miss?" a coarse male voice asked her urgently.

"The light in my eyes," she managed to reply, and the strong flashlight was withdrawn.

"We thought you was gone for sure," the owner of the voice said. She saw now he was a short, over-weight man in a white smock and a black beret.

"That's a fact," a second voice chimed in. She stared up and saw what could only be described as a twin of the first man. He also wore a white smock and a black beret.

She struggled to get up, and the men assisted her. "How did you know?" she asked.

The first man told her, "We were at the festival, same as everyone else. Then we saw this bloke dancing off down the alley with you. Looked a bit on the queer side, it did. And when we heard you scream, we knew something was wrong, so we came running."

"Did you see my attacker?"

"Just saw him nipping over the wall," the second man said. "He got away good and clear."

"We're a couple of Englishmen here on a holiday," the first man said. "That's why we're in these costumes. Never trust foreigners, is my motto."

"Thank you," she said sincerely. "You saved my life."

"Any idea who the bloke was?" he wanted to know.

"None," she said. There was no point in trying to explain about Romitelli and his motives to these strangers.

"Can we help you back to your hotel?" the second man asked.

"I'll see," she told them, trying to straighten out her dress. "I have some friends with me here. They'll want to help me."

The first man said meaningfully, "I'd say you needed some friends, miss."

They escorted her up the dark alley to the festival. People were still dancing in a circle; laughter and good-natured talk filled the air. It was as if nothing had changed under the colorful lights and party atmosphere.

Then a man in a sheik's flowing robes and headdress came up to her. He spoke, and she recognized Tom Clarendon's voice. "You look upset, Trudy. What has happened?"

"Plenty, Guv," one of the Englishmen volunteered. "Some nasty bloke dragged her down into the alley and tried to attack her. Me and my chum came along just in time to save her."

"Is this true?" Tom asked in alarm.

"Yes," she said. "Have you seen Carl or Sylvia?"

"Not for the last ten minutes or so. They were dancing together, and then there was no sign of them."

Trudy anxiously searched the circle of dancers to try to get a glimpse of them. "They must be here!" she cried.

"You came with them, of course," Tom said.

"Yes."

"I'll take you home, don't worry."

"You'll look after the lady, then?" the first Englishman asked.

Tom nodded. "And thank you very much for helping my friend."

"All in the line of duty," the second man told him. Then he smiled at Trudy and said, "You watch your step, miss."

"I will. Please don't let me spoil your evening."

"Not likely." He winked at her. "We've still got a lot of drinking to do." He and his friend ambled off to the line at the wine bar.

"Who was it?" Tom asked her as soon as they were alone.

"The masked swordsman," she said bitterly.

"I don't believe it!"

"First disguised as a monk. He discarded the robe when he attacked me."

"Romitelli!" Tom looked about angrily. "You know he came here dressed as a monk."

"I thought of him," she said. "But there are a lot of others wearing that same costume."

"The main thing is to get you back home."

"I should wait for Sylvia and Carl," she protested.

"It might mean waiting a long time. I'll take you."

"What about Lena?"

"She's here with some other people. She won't miss me before I get back."

He led her away from the noisemakers to where his car was parked. Soon she was being whisked through the countryside to Castle Malice.

Tom had removed the headdress and mask, and the moon coming in through the car windows lit up his face. She could see that he was still in an angry mood.

Glancing at her, he said, "If it was Romitelli, he must be made to pay."

"Let's not do anything rash," she cautioned. "Let's be sure before we make a move."

"You could have been killed tonight."

"I know."

"I can read it all," Tom said grimly. "Romitelli has to be the one whose name is in that will."

"He says he's not."

Tom showed surprise. "You've discussed this with him?"

"Yes," Trudy said. "I promised him I wouldn't tell anyone, but I decided later that I could confide in you."

"You can certainly trust me with anything."

"I know that," she said. "Adrian says he isn't the heir and that Aunt Julia told him who is."

"He said that?"

"Yes. And he hinted that he intended to blackmail whoever it might be."

Tom's disbelief was etched in his expression and in his voice. "I think that was a story made up for your benefit—to put you off guard. I still say he's the one named after you."

Trudy sighed, feeling weary and shaken after her ordeal. "I don't know," she admitted. "You could be right. I've discovered I'm no match for the deviousness I've found here."

They arrived at the entrance to Castle Malice, and Tom brought her to the door.

"You'd better hurry back before Lena misses you," she said, feeling guilty about taking him away from the festival.

"I'm not her lapdog," Tom informed her.

"I know that, but you did take her to the party."

"Will you be safe now?" he asked worriedly.

"Yes."

"I want to talk with you tomorrow about many things. I'll pick you up around eleven, and we'll go to the beach."

"I think I'll be feeling well enough by then," she said.

"I'll come by in any case," he said, his eyes boring into hers. Then he took her in his arms and kissed her several times. Her heartbeat quickened, and she pressed against him with a tiny sob of relief.

"I needed you so," she murmured.

"Send for me whenever you like. I intend to see you through this."

"I feel like running away from it all."

"No, that's not the solution. We'll talk about it in the morning. And avoid Romitelli!"

She smiled wryly. "You don't have to offer that warning."

"Now I must go back." Tom gave her a quick kiss before rushing off to his car.

The great castle was quiet. No one was in sight. Trudy assumed that Benson Steiburn had gone to bed and that Sylvia and Carl had not yet returned. She wondered what had happened to them and could only assume they had gone off on another lovers' tryst. They'd felt she would be kept busy at the festival and would not notice their absence. It hadn't turned out that way.

The horror of being trapped in the dark alley with the masked swordsman still tormented her. She slowly prepared for bed, then took a warm shower and a sleeping tablet to ensure that she wouldn't lie awake for hours worrying.

When she went downstairs for breakfast the next morning, Sylvia was still at the breakfast table. "I've been so worried about you!" she said. "Where did you vanish to last night?"

"Tom brought me home."

"So that's how it was. As soon as I returned, I stopped by your room and opened the door enough to see that you were in bed and asleep. I didn't bother you then."

"Where is Carl?" Trudy asked.

"He and my father are off to Rome for a day or two. I think part of their business on the trip has to do with your inheritance."

"I see," Trudy said, sipping her coffee. "Something rather unpleasant happened last night."

"What are you saying?"

Trudy told her, ending with, "I'm not certain it was Adrian. But I have grave suspicions about him."

"You should have," Sylvia agreed. "He obviously tried to murder you!"

"I can't prove that," Trudy protested.

"Who else was dressed as a monk?"

"A number of people."

"But none we know," the other woman hastened to say. "The little monster! We should never have accepted him—he's not our kind of person. He may well have murdered your aunt, as well!"

Trudy sat back in her chair and sighed. "I don't know what to do. I'd hoped that Carl would be here this morning to advise me."

"It is unfortunate he's away."

"I'll just have to wait until he returns, I guess."

"You must be especially careful in the meantime," Sylvia warned her.

"I intend to be."

"Don't go anywhere alone."

"I won't," she said. "Tom is picking me up this morning, and we're going to the beach for a swim."

Sylvia nodded. "You should be safe with him."

"I never worry when he's with me. He's really very nice."

"Too nice to be tied to Lena Morel."

Trudy's eyebrows raised. "Do you think there is anything more between them than his doing her biography?"

"He's living with her."

"But many people here have house guests. I'm one myself."

"I hope for his sake you're right" was Sylvia's comment.

They did not pursue the subject further.

Later she went up and put on her crimson bikini, her beach dress and the straw hat. She'd barely reached the front entrance when Tom arrived.

"I was afraid you wouldn't make it," he said as he helped her into his car.

She smiled wryly. "I'm famous for bouncing back from unpleasant incidents."

"I know few girls who could manage it as well as you do."

"Did you get back before Lena missed you?" she asked.

"She had a lot of wine and was with an old friend. She didn't even know I'd left." He headed down the road to the highway.

"Good. Carl and Sylvia were very concerned until they found I was safely back at the castle."

"They should have been," Tom said indignantly.

"Carl is away today, so I wasn't able to tell him what happened. I did tell Sylvia."

"I'm sure it was Romitelli."

"It seems so," she agreed. "I'll wait until Carl and Mr. Steiburn return before I take any action."

"I hope that won't be too late," Tom worried. "Romitelli could run off any time. He has no real ties here."

Trudy closed her eyes and sat back. "Please, let's not talk about it anymore. Let us enjoy the morning."

"Sorry," he apologized. Little more was said until they reached the deserted beach area where they had been before.

Trudy stepped from the car and surveyed the white expanse of sand, the tall palm trees with patches of grass around them, and the emerald-blue ocean tinged with silver flecks from the sun. She took a deep breath of air and turned impulsively to Tom. "This could be a paradise! Why do the people here have to spoil it?"

Tom was removing his white pullover. His torso was bronzed and muscular. "You could say the same thing about many places. It's part of the human tragedy."

After they'd put down the blanket, Trudy removed her beach dress and began to apply lotion to protect her from the harmful rays of the sun.

Seated beside her in white trunks, which set off his tanned body perfectly, Tom smiled and said, "You look more beautiful today than I've ever seen you."

"Call it beach illusion," she said. "We all tend to look our best here."

Tom was the first one in the water. He dived straight in and swam about vigorously, while Trudy made a rather timid effort to join him. She waded in first and then, after spending some time standing in water hip-deep, she struck out toward him. They swam together and thoroughly enjoyed themselves.

Later, as they rested on the blanket, he told her, "You know, you swim very well."

"As well as Lena?"

"Better, I'd say." He pointed toward the horizon and went on. "Remember that raft I told you about? I'd love it if we swam out there together."

She smoothed back some of her water-splashed hair and said, "I don't think I could manage it."

"I think you could. There'd be no risk. I'd be at your side all the time. And it's a wonderful thrill to make it out there."

She gazed at the horizon. "The raft seems so far away."

"It's really not. But it's so small you can't see it too well from here. The very best time to try to reach it is near dusk."

"Near dusk?" she repeated, somewhat surprised.

"Yes, because of the movement of the tides and because there's no sun to blind you. The ocean is still warm enough in the early evening."

"I'll take your word for it," she said.

He reached over and took her hand in his. "I want us to go out there one evening. It will be another bond between us."

She laughed. "Aren't we close enough as it is?"

"Not quite," he said seriously. "I want you to be my wife, Trudy. You must have guessed that."

Trudy withdrew her hand. "Tom, this is a poor time to discuss such things. I'm too mixed up."

He turned from her to stare out at the ocean. "It's still Carl Redman, isn't it?"

"Why do you say that?"

"I think it's true." He glanced back at her. "Can you tell me you're not in love with our doctor?"

"I don't think you should ask such questions, and I certainly don't think I should answer them."

His smile was grim. "You've given me my answer. You're still hoping Carl is interested in you."

"I like many things about him—just as I like you when you're not in this mood," she replied.

He leaned toward her and said earnestly, "You must have seen that Carl and Sylvia are lovers. It's only a matter of time before she announces she's leaving her husband and is going to marry him."

"I will believe that when I hear it from one of them."

He laughed mirthlessly. "You're asking to be hurt, Trudy. I want to save you from heartbreak."

"I'm sure your intentions are the best," Trudy told him. "But what about the gossip I hear concerning you and Lena?"

Tom frowned. "That's vicious nonsense. There's nothing to it!"

"Yet some people believe it."

"Lena and I are not even all that friendly. We have plenty of rows."

"What about?"

"A lot of things," he said disgustedly. "She's never satisfied with the way I write the book. And she blames me because your aunt didn't leave her anything in the will."

"How can she possibly do that?"

Tom shrugged and curled and uncurled a towel in his strong hands. "She says that I gave Julia the impression I was going to stay with her when the book was finished and look after her. That way she wouldn't need anything."

"Did you give my aunt that impression?"

"I surely didn't intend to, but you know how people sometimes interpret things the way they want to."

"So now everything depends on the success of the book."

He nodded. "And the way Lena's been behaving, I may never be able to finish it. I've written some sections over and over again. When I want to question her about some details, she locks herself in her room and won't talk to me."

Trudy was surprised to hear this. "But that's only hurting herself!"

He grimaced. "She's been doing that most of her life. Aside from her getting older, it's one of the main reasons she has no film offers. Most people she worked with found her so difficult they never wanted to hire her again."

"Have you thought of giving up the project?"

"A lot," he said. "I may do it yet."

Trudy hadn't realized the desperation of his plight. Like all the others, she had assumed that Lena was a willing and helpful collaborator on her biography. But obviously this was not the case. Nor was Tom her lover, as some people had thought; he didn't even seem to like the older woman.

"Is she jealous of your coming here with me?" Trudy asked.

"In a twisted kind of way, yes. It's not a personal jealousy. It's just that she wants power over me—to be able to decide on my comings and goings. And I won't have that."

Trudy decided that she understood why Tom was so anxious to marry her. It would rescue him from the desperate situation in which he found himself. She was an heiress, if only a temporary one, and would be the answer to all his financial problems. He seemed to care genuinely for her, but once again she felt she had to be wary.

Rising, she put on her beach dress and said, "Please take me back now, Tom. I'm tired."

He got to his feet and faced her solemnly. "Will you give my offer serious consideration?"

"Your offer?"

"Of marriage," he said.

She nodded. "Yes, of course."

He said no more, but she could sense a heaviness mixed with disappointment in his mood as he drove her back to Castle Malice. In an effort to lighten things a little, she leaned over and kissed him briefly before she left the car.

As she walked toward the door, he called after her, "We'll get together again and swim to the raft."

She turned around and smiled. "I'll get myself in the mood for it." Then she waved him on his way.

Inside, she met only one of the maidservants and thought it likely that Sylvia had gone off somewhere. She climbed the stairs to her room and immediately took off her bikini and got into the shower. She had enjoyed the beach, but her pleasure had been marred slightly by the intensity of Tom's manner as he'd declared his love for her. She wished it had come at some other time and under happier circumstances.

Trudy was in a restless mood. She went downstairs and had a light lunch alone. The elderly housekeeper informed her that Sylvia had gone to spend the day with a friend in Lerici. So she was completely on her own.

She strolled in the rose gardens and suddenly had an impulse to get away from the castle. Since there was always a small sports car at the disposal of the guests, she went to the garage and obtained the keys.

Without planning to, she began driving along the road that led to Palina. It was a lovely, sunny afternoon, and she enjoyed the various sights along the way. She passed an old man with a donkey cart, then met an old woman carrying a huge basket and halted to let her cross the road.

As she entered the village, some young men—stripped to the waist and working on road repairs—waved and whistled at her. She continued on into the village itself, which looked much less attractive and colorful than it had last night. The local folk were busy taking the lanterns down from the trees, wires and building fronts. Trudy found a place to park her car, then took a short walk around the tiny cobblestoned area.

It puzzled her that she had made this pilgrimage. She could only put it down to boredom. Tired of being alone at the castle, she had made her way here. As she moved from spot to spot, she suddenly came upon the alley down which she had fled. She stared into its darkness with a perverse sort of fascination.

And then, like a person in a trance, she found herself slowly moving forward. She had gone only a few steps when she saw something that made her stop and gasp. She bent down and picked up a red clown's hat—the identical hat that Carl had been wearing the previous night!

CHAPTER THIRTEEN

"ARE YOU COLLECTING clown hats?" a familiar cynical voice asked. "If so, you must collect some of mine."

She gasped and looked up from the bedraggled hat into the bleakly smiling face of Adrian Romitelli. The sight of him standing there coolly in a white suit with his shirt collar open at the neck left her bereft of words.

He continued to startle her by saying, "Why do you look so frightened? I'm not the masked swordsman!"

Finally she exclaimed, "You were here last night!"

"Wrong!"

"Here in this same alley," she said. "I'm certain of it."

"I fear the sun or the wine has addled your brain," he went on smoothly. "I did not attend the festival last night. I was nowhere near here."

She clutched the hat and stared at him, wide-eyed. "You weren't here?" she echoed.

"No, my dear Trudy, I was not. A friend of mine from Genoa showed up, and we went on to Lerici for an all-night tour of the bars. Along the way I encountered your lawyer, Giuseppe Pascal, though I suspect he was too deep in his cups to recognize me."

She found his story hard to believe. "You say you were in Lerici all night?"

"I do," he replied. "This morning my friend dropped me off here and went back to Genoa. I hope he arrives safely."

"But I saw you," she insisted. "You were wearing a monk's costume."

"Please try to understand," Adrian said with exaggerated patience. "I was not here, with or without a monk's costume, since I didn't attend the ball at all."

She stared at the clown's hat and murmured, "So it was someone else." A dreadful suspicion was crossing her mind that it might indeed have been Carl. He could have worn the swordsman outfit under his bulky clown costume. A moment would be all he would have needed to shed his outer garment. Along the way he'd dropped the clown's hat, which might be her only clue to who her attacker had been.

"I'm sure I don't know what you mean by someone else," Adrian said. "But I must tell you that you look ill, as if you might faint."

"I must get out of this alley," she said weakly.

"Let me help you," he offered solicitously.

Her mind was reeling from the revelations of the last few moments. The whole realm of possibilities had been subtly changed. Carl's mysterious disappearance of last night fitted in with his impersonating the ghost. But he could not have done it without Sylvia's knowledge and support.

"Feeling better now?" Adrian asked.

"A little," she said.

"There's a tavern across the square—a favorite of mine," he said. "Let us go there and have some wine.

I need a drink badly, and judging from the way you look, so do you.''

She did not argue with him, and allowed him to guide her to a small building with some tables in front of it. They sat down at one of the tables, and a portly waiter appeared immediately.

Adrian gave his order to the man, then said to Trudy, ''You look a little silly sitting there with that dirty hat clutched to you.''

''I must keep it,'' she said. ''I have a reason.''

''Indeed,'' he said, arching an eyebrow. ''Well, I seldom question a female about her reasons.''

Their wine was brought out, and after she took a few sips, she felt better. ''The other day you told me you knew the name of the person named in Aunt Julia's second will.''

He frowned. ''I also asked you not to mention it again, for your safety and mine.''

''I'm thinking of that,'' she said. ''We could both be in danger.''

''You must not repeat what I said to anyone,'' he warned her.

She knew she'd already told Tom, but that didn't worry her, since she could rely on him. She made no mention of this to Adrian but said, ''Do you truly have that information?''

''Yes,'' he said smugly.

Trudy hesitated. ''Is it possible that Aunt Julia would name Carl in her will? He once asked her to marry him, or so I've been told.''

''Your aunt was a perverse woman. She could have named anyone from me to Lena Morel to the charming Dr. Redman.''

"You know and you won't tell me!"

"That is right," he replied. "It is for my protection and yours. You are safer not to know."

"Lena Morel blames Tom because my aunt didn't include her in the will. She claims Aunt Julia felt Tom was her lover and would look after her."

"It's possible," he said, "though I would not think it's true. Lena is a difficult older woman, a woman without any prospects. And Tom Clarendon is ambitious."

"How close were Lena and my aunt?"

"They were friends one day and fought the next." Adrian shrugged. "You know how it is with older women."

"I'm afraid I don't," she said coolly. "You sound as if you liked neither of them."

"That is correct. I have few friends I admire."

"Perhaps that's why you do not inspire friendship in others," she told him.

"Don't chastise me, dear Trudy," he said, waving to the waiter for more wine. "It is terribly plebian on your part and doesn't become you."

She faced him directly across the table. "You must know that many people think you are the one who's in that second will."

He smiled. "Let them think what they like."

"They also think you were mixed up in my aunt's mysterious drowning."

"That is too far-fetched for even you to believe!"

"And that you are therefore a threat to me."

He shook his head. "I have great admiration for you. You are one of the few people I enjoy being with on the tennis court."

She downed some more wine and then managed a faint smile. "You are a rogue, but at times I find myself liking you."

He spread his hands. "Even rogues have their good points."

"I hope so," she said. "I may still need your help."

"Always at your service," he assured her. "For a price, of course."

"Those terms are acceptable," she agreed.

He saw her to her car and waved after her as she drove off. The journey back to the castle found her in a strange frame of mind. It seemed fantastic, but during the short period of this one afternoon, all the dark doubts she'd had about Adrian Romitelli had been dispersed. True, she knew him to be the scoundrel he did not deny he was. But she could no longer think of him as anything worse than a possible blackmailer. She'd even told him about her attack and how the Englishmen had saved her. She felt he was sincere in his feelings for her—shallow though they were—and that she and the others had done him a grave injustice by thinking of him as murderer.

Yet he did have information that someone who was a murderer must want badly. Unless he'd merely been boasting to her without any certain knowledge to back up his talk. But she didn't think that was true. She believed he had been told that fateful name by her aunt.

Now it seemed that Carl Redman had to take his place high among her suspects. What his motives might be were too complicated for her to understand. If he had Sylvia and the Steiburn fortune within his grasp, why should he murder to gain her aunt's estate? It did not seem logical, yet there might be some reason, if only a result of the workings of a sick mind. The bedraggled clown hat lay next to her on the car seat, surely an accusing piece of evidence.

Back at the castle, Trudy changed into a modest brown dinner dress. When she went downstairs, she saw that Sylvia had returned. The lovely dark woman was wearing a bright green gown with a plunging neckline. From her ears dangled long diamond earrings that Trudy thought must be worth a fortune; her neck was graced with a diamond pendant that looked equally expensive.

"Forgive me if I've overdressed when dinner is just for the two of us. But I feel depressed if I don't look my best in the evening."

Feeling like a forlorn brown bird in the face of Sylvia's elegance, Trudy managed a weak smile. "I'm afraid I'm the one who failed the occasion."

"I can understand, after last night's dreadful ordeal!"

"I went back there today."

Sylvia was astonished. "Why would you do that?"

"Some sort of impulse, I guess."

"I'm not sure I understand," Sylvia told her. "But I found out something today that will interest you. I heard it in Lerici."

"Yes?" She thought she already knew what Sylvia was going to tell her.

"It's very strange. I met Giuseppe Pascal at the restaurant where my friend and I were having lunch. He told me he saw Romitelli in Lerici last night, so he couldn't have been at the festival."

"I know," Trudy said quietly.

"You do?"

"Adrian told me himself. I met him in the village today—in the very alley where I was attacked."

"That's incredible!" Sylvia exclaimed. "So your monk could not have been Romitelli!"

"No. We've been unfair to him."

"With good reason. He's such a bounder, hangs on here, where he isn't wanted, and owes everyone money."

"Yet I don't see him as a murderer," Trudy said.

Sylvia stared at her. "Then who?"

"I'm not sure," she said bitterly. "But someone is enjoying playing the role of the masked swordsman."

"So we're back where we began."

"Not quite." And then she revealed the battered hat she'd been holding behind her back. "Do you recognize this?" she asked.

Sylvia took it from her and examined the inside of the hat. "It's the one Carl wore last night," she said. "I can tell by the name of the costumer. He bought it in Rome."

"It was in the alley," Trudy said.

"Yes, I believe that," Sylvia agreed rather nervously.

"Can you think how it got there?"

"That I don't know," Sylvia said, passing the hat back to her. "But I do know that Carl took it off when we sat down for some wine, and when he looked for it a few minutes later, it was gone. Someone had taken it."

Trudy raised her eyebrows. "You're telling me someone stole that hat from Carl?"

"Yes."

"You didn't say anything about it earlier."

"I didn't think it was important," Sylvia said. "Especially after hearing your story."

Very deliberately, Trudy said, "The hat has something to do with my story. I found it in the alley where I was attacked."

Sylvia looked more upset than she had before. She spoke in a near whisper. "Surely you don't think—" But she didn't finish her sentence.

"I hardly know what I dare think," Trudy replied, gazing at the hat. "You have come up with such a convenient explanation—that it had been stolen."

"It's true," Sylvia insisted. "Carl will tell you when he returns."

"I'm certain he will," Trudy said with irony.

"Carl was with me almost all the time."

"Almost?"

"He did leave me for a short while," Sylvia said unhappily. "He went looking for you."

"I wonder why he didn't find me." She paused. "Or could it be that he did?"

"Please don't say such things. Carl could never harm you. Or anyone. He's one of the most gentle people I know."

Trudy felt no good could come of a further discussion at that point, so she said, "I think we should have dinner now."

They sat, two lone women, at the huge dining room table that could accommodate twenty-four. Their chairs were opposite each other at the head of the table. Candlelight gave the white linen tablecloth and the silverware and china a gentle illumination.

A manservant moved noiselessly about, serving them the various courses and pouring suitable wine for each. In the quiet atmosphere it was only natural that the women should relax. As they left the dining room together after the meal, much of their tensions had vanished.

In the living room, Sylvia sat in one of the high-backed chairs. Trudy remained standing by the fireplace, partly turned to her.

"Father and Carl will be back the day after tomorrow," Sylvia said. "I can hardly wait for their return."

"I understand," Trudy said.

Sylvia leaned forward in her chair. "There is something I must say to you."

Trudy made a small gesture. "No more explanations are necessary."

"This has nothing to do with last night. It's about something else."

"Oh?" Trudy wondered what might be coming next. Sylvia was trying so hard to convince her that Carl could not have had anything to do with the attack on her.

Sylvia's clasped hands moved nervously, and she stared down at them. "What I'm going to say is about me and Carl."

"No explanations are needed," Trudy said again.

"I think they are," Sylvia said, looking up at her now. "I'm sure you believe Carl and I are having an affair."

"It's none of my business."

"I want you to know the truth. My husband and I had a quarrel. I was considering leaving him and that is why I have stayed on here."

"It doesn't matter."

"I think it does. It's true I was in love with Carl, and I briefly considered going back to him. But that isn't going to happen. My husband and I are reconciled, and I will be returning to New York next week."

Trudy wondered if Sylvia was telling the truth or making a desperate effort to quiet Trudy's suspicions of the man Sylvia loved. Under other circumstances, Trudy knew she would have welcomed this confession and been happy to accept it. Even now, in her total confusion, she was very attracted to Carl.

"So you know the truth," Sylvia said, "and I feel better for having told you. For a while there, I hoped you and Carl had found something in each other."

"Too much uncertainty," Trudy said.

"You need have none about Carl," Sylvia insisted. "He has been disturbed by your coldness toward him lately. We both feared it was because you felt we were having a secret affair."

Trudy decided to combat this in her own way. As calmly as she could, she said, "If I have formed any romantic attachment since coming here, it is for Tom Clarendon."

The bluntness of her statement took Sylvia by surprise. "Tom?" she said, her eyes wide.

"Yes. And there's nothing definite settled between us, though there very well could be."

Sylvia nodded. "Well, if you love him and he loves you, I hope you'll be happy together. It's not easy to find the right man. I know from experience."

"I hope you'll be happy, as well," Trudy replied in the same spirit.

A little later on, Trudy was touched when Sylvia paused at the head of the stairs and kissed her good-night. Then they each went their separate ways to their rooms. Trudy was in a troubled, mixed-up mood as she prepared for bed. She wanted to believe every-thing Sylvia had told her, but she couldn't be sure.

Someone had attacked her the previous night. It was no longer possible that the person had been Adrian Romitelli. Finding Carl's hat in the alley had to make her suspicious of him. And she would continue to feel that way until the identity of the masked swordsman was revealed.

Sleep did not come quickly. Aside from the ser-vants, she and Sylvia were alone in the huge mansion, and that bothered her. With its many entrances, Cas-tle Malice was an ideal spot for ghostly appearances.

At last sheer exhaustion won out over nervous dis-tress. Trudy fell into a light sleep that was peopled by phantom figures. Once again she saw the gypsy woman whose path she'd crossed in Genoa; then the looming shape of the masked swordsman stalked across the stage of her nightmare. The figure came close to her and lifted its mask to reveal the sneering face of Carl. Trudy moaned and turned restlessly in the bed, making a turmoil of the sheets.

When she awakened, it was morning. All at once she became aware of a strange smell in the room. It took her a moment to recognize it, and when she did, a chill ran through her. The scent of wild violets lingered in the air around her.

She recalled Adrian Romitelli's claim that the spirit of her aunt had visited him and left him a message in the form of a handkerchief with her initials on it. Had Trudy had the same sort of visitation? Had her aunt come to her with a message?

Staring about her, she saw a piece of paper on the bed covering. With a trembling hand, she reached for it. It was a sheet of her aunt Julia's engraved notepaper, and written on it in Julia's handwriting were the words "Dear Trudy." She held the paper up to her nose and smelled the perfumed scent of wild violets.

Since Sylvia was the only other person in the house, aside from the servants, Trudy immediately thought of her as the possible culprit. This made sense if Carl were Trudy's other arch enemy and Sylvia was secretly working with him. Yet she knew she couldn't jump to such a conclusion. She had been hasty in condemning Adrian and had been wrong about him. It was quite possible that someone from outside had played this grisly trick on her.

In the end, she decided to say nothing about it and hoped that if Sylvia were involved, she might somehow give herself away. It was a risk worth taking.

By the time she came downstairs, Sylvia had already eaten breakfast and had gone off to visit a friend at one of the beach estates. Trudy had breakfast alone and then went out into the garden to read and try to sort things out in her mind. She'd only been there for a half hour when she heard the sound of a car. She got up and saw Lena Morel's shabby black sedan come to a halt in the driveway.

Lena, wearing a taupe summer suit, got out of the car with an air of jaunty self-assurance and a very determined look on her face.

Trudy went out to greet her. "I'm afraid I'm the only one here. Were you looking for Mr. Steiburn or Sylvia?"

"Either one would have done," Lena said crisply. "As it is, I'll settle for a scotch and water with you."

"Do sit down. I'll get it for you."

A few minutes later she came back with a scotch for the actress and a mineral water for herself. Lena took a big swallow of the strong drink and smiled. "Best way to begin the day," she said. "When you reach my age, you'll know that."

Trudy sat down opposite her. "I'm sorry the others aren't here."

"It doesn't matter," Lena said. Then she gave Trudy a sharp look. "You've been swimming again with Tom."

"Yes," she said, not sure she liked the other woman's tone.

Lena smiled coldly. "I hope you aren't getting ideas about him."

Trudy found herself blushing, to her annoyance. "Ideas?" she echoed.

"You know what I mean," the older woman said. "Tom has charm and can't help using it. The trouble is, I don't think he has any future for a girl like you."

Trudy did not bother to conceal her resentment. "I think I can best decide that for myself."

Lena Morel's smile was mocking. "Your aunt Julia would not approve."

"What makes you so certain of that?"

"I knew her better than most people did—that's why."

"And perhaps thanks to her friendship with you, she is dead," Trudy said, rising.

Lena Morel went white and jumped up. "Did Tom tell you that?"

"No," Trudy said bitterly. "But I've heard it from almost everyone else."

"How dare you talk to me like that, you little nothing!" Lena flared. "Julia never cared a fig about you or any of your family. She simply made you her heir because she wanted to revenge herself on me."

"Thank you," Trudy said politely. "Would you be kind enough to leave? I have a splitting headache."

"You'll have more than a headache before you're finished here!" Lena sneered. Then she turned and stalked off to her car.

Tears filled Trudy's eyes as she watched Lena's car hurtle away. The actress had a vicious tongue. It was clear that Lena hated her for more than one reason— because she had won Julia's legacy, and because Lena realized Tom was ready to give up on her and the book. Perhaps he had openly declared he'd fallen in love.

No matter what had prompted Lena Morel's visit, it was certain that the older woman hated her. She could not forget that several people questioned the part Lena had played in Julia's death. Would they one day be speculating on the same thing about her own demise?

CHAPTER FOURTEEN

PARTLY BECAUSE TRUDY was haunted by the lingering aroma of wild violets from the previous night's visitation, and partly because Lena Morel's venomous behavior had reinforced the mystery surrounding her aunt Julia's death, she found herself drawn to the villa and the pool.

She stood silently in the shadow of the old building whose key she now possessed, but had no desire to explore it again. She was at the point where she felt that the best solution would be to strip it of its treasures and then, if possible, sell it to Benson Steiburn. Perhaps peace would come to the entire area if the villa were destroyed.

Or would the macabre spirit of the masked swordsman merely retreat to Castle Malice and continue its evil? Surely whoever was pursuing her was a masquerader bent on murder. If she could successfully bring him to justice, the whole myth of the masked swordsman would come to an end.

Staring down into the leave-strewn, stagnant pool, which had not been used since her aunt's body had been found in it, she saw her own murky likeness reflected in the water. At that moment, it seemed as if she'd have to challenge Carl about playing the role of the masked swordsman.

Her thoughts were interrupted by the sound of a car approaching. She left the pool and walked toward the roadway in time to see Tom emerge from the car. His shirt was open at the neck, and he was wearing a pair of yellow work pants. His face was pale, and his hands were clenched at his sides as he came up to her.

"She was here," he said tautly.

"You mean Lena," Trudy said, troubled to see him looking so upset.

"She said she'd called on you," the writer continued in the same fashion. "I told her it was the last straw. I've left her *and* the book!"

"Is that wise?"

"It's the only way for me. I've borrowed this car from a friend and I'm moving into his beach house. I have an assignment from a New York agency to do a series of articles on the Italian Riviera. I'll be my own man again."

"If that's what you want, I'm glad for you."

"I've never been so unhappy as during these past few months," Tom said. "I had no idea Lena would be foolish enough to be jealous of you. It's better that it came out. Now she knows I love you and want to marry you."

Trudy smiled, a small smile. "Let's not hurry things, Tom. Get yourself adjusted to your new life first. There's plenty of time for us."

"I'm afraid of losing you," he said earnestly, taking her by the arm.

"I don't think that's likely to happen now."

He drew her to him and kissed her for a long, throbbing moment. The ardent embrace left her feeling a trifle weak.

He released her and said, "I wanted to let you know what's going on with me. I'll be in touch again soon. I want us to swim out to the raft at dusk." His face brightened for the first time since he'd arrived. "I've imagined us out there alone, the monarchs of our own little world."

After he'd driven away, Trudy felt as confused as she had felt earlier. It pleased her that he had escaped from the domination of the tyrannical Lena. She was sure he was better off on his own. But she knew this meant he would be more insistent about their future together. Though she was fond of him, she had apprehensions about committing herself to anyone just then. Rather shamefacedly, she wondered if the reason was that she couldn't dispel her feelings for Carl.

The balance of that day and evening passed without anything untoward happening. She and Sylvia dined together again and afterward spent some time talking about New York and other things back in the States. Sylvia had discreetly avoided any mention of Carl, and so had Trudy.

The next morning Carl and Benson Steiburn arrived back in time for everyone to have breakfast together. Trudy said nothing to disturb the pleasant mood of their return. After the meal Steiburn took her aside for a short talk.

"I've been over the entire business of the will with my attorneys," he said. "It is their opinion that the will cannot be broken but that it might be modified."

"Modified?" she questioned.

He stroked his beard and explained. "By that I mean it might be altered slightly on appeal, so that you would receive some permanent benefits for your own estate—such as the proceeds of a possible sale of the villa."

"But the second will must otherwise stand?"

"That is what they think," Steiburn said. "You can't be sure, of course, until you go through the courts. But the future looks better for you than we thought."

"Thank you for your efforts," she said.

He took her hands in his and clasped them warmly. "The work will go on," he promised.

"I've just about decided to sell the villa to you. I think I'll feel better if it is leveled."

"I would call it a wise move, my dear. It was one of the few points on which Julia and I differed."

With that settled, Trudy waited for a chance to speak with Carl. She found him eventually, seated at the desk in the library, and placed the red clown's hat in front of him.

He stood up awkwardly. "Sylvia told me that you'd found the hat."

"I expected she would," Trudy said, studying him closely.

Carl bit his lower lip. "You can't think I had anything to do with the attack on you."

"I don't know *what* to think!"

"Aside from the idea being ridiculous, what possible motive could I have to harm you?"

She sighed. "Perhaps you are my heir, the one my aunt named in that second will."

Carl stared at her incredulously. "You know that's nonsense!"

"No one knows the name in that will, with the possible exception of Adrian. And I doubt if he really does know."

Carl frowned. "I don't care where Romitelli was the night of the ball. I think he's the man to watch. It could be a simple matter of his timing it so that he was at the festival, then quickly drove to Lerici to be seen there and have a perfect alibi."

She realized this was a possibility. But she had a conviction, based on intuition, that it wasn't. She might be naive, but she thought of Adrian as her friend.

Nothing could be settled at this point, so she said, "I just wanted to return your hat."

"Thank you," he said grimly. "It's not worth much."

Her eyes met his as she replied, "Yet I'm sure you'll feel better with it in your own hands." And she went out, leaving him standing there holding the battered hat.

That evening they all gathered in the living room for after-dinner drinks. Benson Steiburn held the floor, telling them about some new and interesting pieces of sculpture he had just purchased.

Then Romitelli made one of his unexpected appearances. "The French doors were open, so I came in. I was afraid to risk the servants at the front door, since you may have ordered them not to let me in."

Steiburn gazed at him with amused tolerance and said, "You must join us for a whiskey or two."

Romitelli bowed to his host. "I never refuse your noted hospitality." Then he crossed the room to Trudy and asked, "Are you feeling better?"

She summoned a smile. "Somewhat."

"Well, surely that is an improvement," he said. Turning to the others, he announced, "You all know she was attacked by the masked swordsman on the night of the costume ball."

"Some fool playing a prank," Steiburn growled.

"I don't agree. If those two men hadn't come along, Trudy would be dead and buried now."

Sylvia shuddered. "Surely we can talk about something more pleasant!"

Carl had poured the whiskey and now handed the drink to Adrian. "This should cheer you up."

"It always has," he said. He raised his glass. "To all of you."

Trudy searched in her mind for something to ease the tension brought on by Adrian's appearance. Then she decided she would try something dramatic.

"I understand that you were once a concert pianist of some note, but I've never heard you play." She indicated the grand piano in the corner of the living room. "Would you be so kind?"

Everyone looked surprised. Adrian merely smiled at her and said, "I believe you genuinely mean that."

"I do."

"Everyone here is aware that I badly injured my right hand playing tennis. I'm not able to approach the piano professionally anymore."

Trudy urged him. "But surely for friends. We do not expect perfection."

Sylvia joined in the effort to convince him to change his mind. "Just play a little something for us."

Romitelli stared at them in silence for a moment; then he put down his glass and crossed to the piano.

He sat down, worked his hands together for a few seconds, then rippled his fingers over the keyboard.

Trudy watched him as he felt out the instrument; she hoped he would not disappoint them. Then he began to play a Beethoven sonata. He bent over the keys lovingly, and everyone in the room listened in rapt silence as he produced a moment of ultimate beauty.

When he'd finished, the silence continued. He closed the cover on the keyboard and rose to go back to his drink. But he was interrupted by a burst of applause from all of them.

Benson Steiburn patted him on the back and said, "You were magnificent! You shouldn't have given it up!"

"I fear the concert masters were the ones who gave *me* up," Adrian said with a bitter smile.

Sylvia and Carl both congratulated him. Then it was Trudy's turn to stand before him and say a quiet "Thanks."

"The best of all words," he said, giving her a rare, warm smile. "Now I must be on my way. I have other calls to make this evening."

Trudy said good-night to him and the others. When she went up to her room, she was in a subdued mood. It seemed wrong to her that a man with his talent should be living as a kind of con man and a blackmailer. She determined to talk to him about this at their next meeting but didn't hold out any hope of changing his outlook.

She slowly prepared for bed, then went over to the window overlooking the balcony and the grounds for a moment. She was just in time to see Adrian stalking across the lawn with that awkward stride of his. His white suit stood out against the darkness.

She went back to finishing applying her night cream and was about to turn off the light when she realized that she hadn't closed the drapes. She'd just put her hand on the curtain pull when she saw a figure step out of the darkness and come close enough to the lights of the castle to be clearly outlined.

It was the masked swordsman. He gazed up at her for a long moment, then vanished into the darkness from which he had emerged.

Trembling, she hastily drew the drapes closed and made her way back to the bed. For a long while she debated what this latest visitation meant and what she might do about it. With nothing resolved, she got into bed and put out the light. It seemed her torment would continue.

WHEN SHE WENT DOWNSTAIRS for breakfast the next morning, she heard a flurry of distressed voices. She entered the breakfast room and saw the others standing there. The expression on their faces as they turned to her let Trudy know something was terribly wrong.

"What is it?" she asked.

Carl glanced at Sylvia and her father, then came over to Trudy. "Another tragedy, I'm afraid."

"What tragedy?"

"Romitelli." Carl paused. "He's dead."

"Dead!" she gasped.

Benson Steiburn came forward to explain. "He killed himself. Threw himself over the cliff near the villa. One of the fishermen found his battered body on the rocks early this morning."

Trudy turned away and pressed her hands to her mouth to stifle her sobs. Sylvia put a comforting arm around her. "You were one of the few who liked him," she said. "And he played so well last night."

Carl said, "Maybe he knew he was at the end of his tether and would be exposed soon. That could be why he killed himself."

Trudy turned around angrily. "Don't tell me you believe that?"

"Why not?" Carl said, shocked at her words.

"He was murdered," she said miserably. "Murdered because he knew who was named in that second will and he tried to blackmail whoever it was!"

Benson Steiburn showed concern. "I wouldn't go around talking like that, my dear. We've had enough scandal here already. The poor fellow took his life. Let it go at that."

She gazed at each of them and knew this was what they wanted to believe. Their silence was her confirmation.

They sat down to breakfast in a sober mood. Carl and his employer carefully kept the conversation on neutral topics. It was only after the meal that Trudy had a chance to talk with Sylvia, who explained that the funeral would be held at a nonsectarian chapel in Lerici and that the body would be buried in the cemetery where Julia had been buried. This was the custom when a member of the foreign colony died in the area. Romitelli was grouped with the colony and, by a grim irony, would rest among their dead.

Trudy made no mention of having seen the masked swordsman. She concluded that his appearance had been a harbinger of Romitelli's death.

On the afternoon of the funeral there was a drenching rainstorm. Benson Steiburn insisted that they all ride with him in the large limousine that was part of his collection of cars. Aside from the priest, they were the only mourners. When the service was over, Trudy heard Steiburn discussing the purchase of a headstone for the unfortunate Romitelli. This was his way of showing goodwill toward the dead man.

That evening Carl came up to her in the living room and said, "I know you're feeling bad about Romitelli, but can you be sure he wasn't your enemy?"

"I'm as sure of that as I will be of anything," she told him wearily.

"I noted that neither Lena Morel nor her friend Tom Clarendon was at the funeral."

"He's no longer her friend. He left her while you were away."

"What about the book?" Carl asked.

"He's given up on it," she said. "He has an assignment from a New York agency to do some articles. He's living with a friend at the beach."

Carl grimaced. "I thought those two were pretty close, that they'd never break up."

"She's been difficult."

"I'd expect that, but still... Did he come here to tell you this?"

"Yes."

"Are you still seeing him at the beach?"

"Yes. He wants me to swim out to the raft with him sometime."

"The raft! He must be crazy! That's too far for anyone but the strongest swimmer."

"He says it isn't so very far and that it's easy to get to when the sea isn't rough."

Carl looked unconvinced. "If you'll take my advice, you won't let him talk you into that."

Trudy paid scant attention to his warning. She believed it was based mostly on his annoyance with her because she still saw Tom now and then. And she intended to go on doing that.

The rain ended during the night, and the following day was warm and sunny. Trudy received a phone call from Tom in the midafternoon, asking her to meet him on the beach around six. "We'll have time to swim to the raft and back, then have dinner in Lerici."

"Is the sea calm?" she asked.

"The sea is perfect! We'll never get a better night."

Later she changed into her swimsuit and left a message for Sylvia that she wouldn't be there for dinner as she was going to swim to the raft and back. Then she drove the small car to the secluded beach. Tom was waiting for her in his bathing trunks.

"You're right on time!" she said with a smile.

"It's the tide," he said. "We have to get it just right."

As she took off her robe, she said, "You know Adrian is dead, don't you?"

"Yes. It's all around the village that he killed himself."

She gazed up at him. "Neither you nor Lena was at the funeral. You both knew him."

"We weren't friends," Tom said. "I don't think he had many."

"I'm beginning to wonder how many friends any of us has," she said, putting on her bathing cap.

Tom put his arm around her. "You have a legion of them. But I want to be the special one."

"When do we start?" she asked.

"Right away," he said. "The tide has just changed."

With an admiring smile on his bronzed face, he led her into the water. He had been right, Trudy thought. The water was pleasantly warm, even though the sun no longer glared overhead.

As they began to swim, he told her, "Stay close to me."

"I will," she promised.

After a little while she glanced over her shoulder. The beach seemed terribly far away. She was beginning to feel weary and thought the swim was endless.

She saw Tom's head bobbing to the left of her and swam a bit harder to get nearer to him. Then, almost breathless, she shouted, "I'm tired!"

He raised a hand to indicate he'd heard her. "We're almost there," he said. "Float for a few minutes and give yourself a rest."

She did, then began the effort again. She was thinking of Carl's advice and decided he'd been right. She couldn't see any sign of the raft, only the constant waves she had to surmount.

"We're home!" Tom shouted and helped her reach the edge of the gently bobbing raft. She pulled herself up onto it and then stared in astonishment at the figure of a woman in a bathing suit.

"Have a good swim?" Lena Morel asked mockingly.

"I didn't expect you to be here!" Trudy gasped, water running down her face and body.

Tom slid up onto the raft and smiled apologetically. "I didn't think you'd mind."

"I don't understand," she said, staring at the two other people on this raft in the middle of nowhere and sensing something was dreadfully wrong.

"I'm here to see that Tom does his job," Lena told her. "He almost lost his nerve last time. If I hadn't been there to direct him, Julia would still be alive."

Tom gave her an angry glance. "That's enough, Lena!"

"It doesn't matter how much more we tell her," Lena said. "She's not going to repeat it."

The full horror of her situation hit Trudy. In a tremulous voice, she cried, "You two!"

Lena's face showed a triumphant smile. "Yes, darling. I'm the one who's named in that second will. Romitelli knew it, so he had to be eliminated, as well."

Trudy hunched back to the edge of the raft, sobbing, "Murderers!"

Tom stared at her uncertainly and then turned to the older woman. She gave him a look of disgust and raised a hand as if to strike him. "Now!" she ordered.

Trudy did not wait for Tom to lurch forward and grasp her. She jumped into the water and literally began swimming for her life. She heard an angry Tom snarl out her name from close behind her. Then he homed in on her and tried to shove her under the water. She fought back silently, directing her attack against his eyes. She clawed at them and found her mark, for he uttered a loud oath and released her.

Free, she swam off again. But he was there behind her. In a matter of seconds he would overtake her and hold her underwater until she drowned—just as he'd done in the pool with her aunt. Later, Trudy's unfortunate drowning would be reported as an accident.

She felt his hands grasp her. At the same moment, she heard the sound of a motorboat. It seemed that Tom heard it as well. He let go of her and began swimming back to the raft. Trudy somehow managed to keep herself afloat until the boat drew up alongside her and she was gently lifted up into it. Choking and spitting out water, she looked up into Carl's troubled face and managed to gasp, "Lena and Tom tried to drown me!"

"I know," he said grimly. He gave the man in charge of the boat some curt instructions, and it closed in on the raft.

Trudy now saw that she was in a police patrol boat, one of several that were used to prevent water accidents at the various beaches. When the uniformed officer ordered Lena and Tom into the big craft, they obeyed abjectly and huddled together in the rear like the criminals they were.

Trudy sat with Carl, who'd wrapped a blanket around her. "How did you know?" she asked.

"You left that message with Sylvia. I was suspicious and fearful, so I called the police and came out with them."

Trudy nestled close to him, no longer tormented with doubts.

Lena Morel and Tom Clarendon were arrested and charged with the murders of Julia and Adrian and the attempted murder of Trudy. The arrest caused a sensation in the village. A few days later Sylvia left for New York and her husband.

Trudy found herself alone at the castle with Carl and Benson Steiburn. A search of Lena's cottage had produced the black outfit of the masked swordsman. It had been Tom, under Lena's direction, who had played the part of the ghost.

One evening Carl and Trudy strolled out to the rose gardens and then over to the villa and the pool. As they stood there in the moonlight, she said, "I'm selling it. It will be torn down."

"It has never been that happy a place," he told her. "As a museum, it will do some good and give everyone pleasure. It will be a fresh beginning."

She looked up at his face, bathed in the moonlight, and said softly, "I think that's what we all need—a fresh beginning."

He put his arms around her and held her close. "Just as long as we have it together."

Explore love with Harlequin in the Middle Ages, the Renaissance, in the Regency, the Victorian and other eras.

Relive within these books the endless ages of romance, set against authentic historical backgrounds. Two new historical love stories published each month.

HIST-A-1

Harlequin Signature Edition

Violet Winspear

THE HONEYMOON

Blackmailed into marriage, a reluctant bride discovers intoxicating passion and heartbreaking doubt.

Is it Jorja or her resemblance to her sister that stirs Renzo Talmonte's desire?

A turbulent love story unfolds in the glorious tradition of Violet Winspear, *la grande dame* of romance fiction.